# Books by Linda Nagata

## Near-Future Science Fiction
*Pacific Storm*
*The Last Good Man*
*Limit of Vision*
*Tech-Heaven*
*The Red Trilogy:*
    *The Red: First Light*
    *The Trials*
    *Going Dark*

## Far-Future Science Fiction
*Inverted Frontier Series:*
    *Edges*
    *Silver*
*The Nanotech Succession:*
    *Tech-Heaven* (prequel)
    *The Bohr Maker*
    *Deception Well*
    *Vast*
*Memory*
*Skye-Object 3270-a (young adult/middle grade)*

## Fantasy Novels
*The Wild Trilogy:*
    *The Snow Chanter*
    *The Long War*
    *Days of Storm*
*Stories of the Puzzle Lands Duology:*
    *The Dread Hammer*
    *Hepen the Watcher*

## Short Fiction Collections
*Light And Shadow: Eight Short Stories*
*Goddesses & Other Stories*

THE WILD TRILOGY: BOOK I

# THE SNOW CHANTER

LINDA NAGATA

Mythic Island Press LLC
Kula, Hawaii

This is a work of fiction. All the characters and events portrayed in this novel are fictitious or are used fictitiously.

*The Snow Chanter*

Copyright © 2021 by Linda Nagata

All rights reserved. No part of this publication may be reproduced, distributed, or transmitted in any form or by any means, including photocopying, recording, or other electronic or mechanical methods, without the prior written permission of the publisher, except in the case of brief quotations embodied in critical reviews and certain other noncommercial uses permitted by copyright law.

ISBN 978-1-937197-35-3

Cover art by Bukovero.com
Cover art copyright © 2021 by Mythic Island Press LLC

Mythic Island Press LLC
P.O. Box 1293
Kula, HI 96790-1293
MythicIslandPress.com

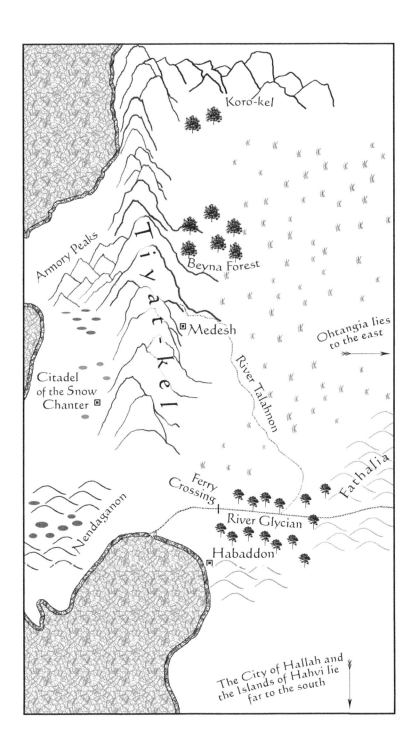

## Prelude: Summer Thunder

All day, the forest had been blanketed by a thick mist that weighed down the meadow grasses. The trees, just shadows. The land, transformed into a puzzle, all its familiar markers hidden.

Lanyon Kyramanthes kept her place halfway back in a long line of riders. She could not see to the front of the column. The horses ahead of her and the hooded warriors astride them faded into invisibility. A saddle creaked, hooves thumped their quiet beat against wet ground. Bird song, soft voices. The annoyed snort of her mare who'd grown increasingly restless, pulling to the right as if determined to take a new direction. The horse's stubborn insistence nurtured Lanyon's doubt. Had their guide become confused? Had the company lost its way in the mist?

Doubt crystallized to certainty with a faint, menacing rumble of faraway thunder. Lanyon pushed back her hood, turned sharply in the saddle. Behind her, more riders, silhouetted in the mist.

Thunder rumbled again. It came from *behind* them, growling down their trail. Again her mare snorted, pulled to the right, but this time, Lanyon did not resist. She let the mare turn, while she called out in a voice meant to be heard at the front of the column, "Jahallon! War Father! We are going the wrong way!"

The warrior behind her reined in his horse with a questioning look. She offered no explanation as she brought her mare around in a full circle to face the oncoming beat of cantering hooves.

Jahallon burst out of the mist, pulled his horse up alongside hers. He eyed the tiny, warm bundle of her newborn daughter asleep in a carrier against her chest. Lanyon's son, who was already one and a half years in the world, was farther back in the line, in the doting care of those women who served as Jahallon's couriers.

"Do you need to stop?" Jahallon asked, sounding puzzled.

"No, War Father."

To the casual eye, he could seem an ordinary man—his broad shoulders might draw notice, or the odd coppery color of his clipped hair; otherwise, he appeared as any warrior in his prime—but this was only the surface of things, the thin skin of creation. Jahallon-the-Undying was bound to a deeper place. Time could not catch him in its current. Alone among the people he could not grow old and he could not die, yet he was loved, not feared, and his willful descendants felt easy enough in his company that they did not hesitate to speak their minds.

"War Father, we have strayed in the mist. I know it. We are going the wrong way."

And after all, Jahallon did not know this land. He had never visited the Citadel of the Snow Chanter, even though the bitter history that had kept him away was long since crumbled to dust. On this, his first journey into the heart of Samokea, he relied on a senior captain to guide the column. But looking at him, Lanyon could see he had doubts, too.

"You're listening to Siddél's thunder?" he asked her.

"Why does it lie behind us? Should we believe the monster has gone south to trouble Habaddon? Or is it more likely Siddél cleaves to custom, growling and threatening from the escarpment of the Tiyat-kel, where no arrows can reach him? He can be heard there almost every afternoon from the ramparts of the Citadel. But that is not all. My horse remembers her home. She fights to turn north ... or what I think is north. I'm certain we're not going north now. We have lost our way."

The riders behind were coming up one by one, gathering around, while those who were ahead had stopped to look back.

Jahallon, too, looked back the way they had come, glaring into the mist as if he could part it merely by the fierceness of his gaze. His age and his long experience had given him a disturbing prescience so that he could foretell an outcome from the least clues, whether on the battlefield or in the hearts of his people. He had also an unrelenting temper.

Fixing his gaze on Lanyon he asked, "Did you summon this mist?"

"*No*," she said in fierce denial. "Why must you think ill of me? Édan is my husband and it was always my intention to return to him."

"You should not have left the Citadel without telling him, when he was gone to war and you with child."

"I have already said I was wrong. I cannot undo it."

How foolish she felt now!

Not so, then, when the cold stone of the Citadel had seemed impervious to the spring. Where was the trickling snowmelt? The glint of new leaves and delicate flowers? The shy face of the sun, lost and found again behind roving clouds? After Édan had gone, such a longing came over her to return for a time to the bright forests of Habaddon, and to visit her friends there, and truly, she meant to stay only a little while. So when a company of couriers set out, she took her son and went with them.

But the campaign dragged on past all expectation. Spring edged into summer and no company could be spared to escort her back to the Citadel. When the army finally did return, Lanyon was so close to term the midwives wouldn't let her undertake the ride. So her daughter wasn't born in the land of Samokea as she should have been, but in Habaddon. Now the infant was twenty-three days old, and though Édan had been back at the Citadel of the Snow Chanter for twice that time, he had not come south to see his daughter, nor sent any word.

"I cannot undo it!" Lanyon said again. "And I am returning to him now—or I would if this mist did not hinder us and set us on false paths."

Jahallon nodded. "I loathe this blind wandering." He lifted his gaze, to address the riders gathered around them. "Let us find a place to raise the tents. We will go no farther until this mist gives way."

Leaving her tiny daughter in the care of the other women, Lanyon took her son walking, letting him play and clamber in the wet grass. She made sure to smile at his antics, though Jahallon's question had added to the dread that already haunted her. *Did you summon this mist?* She had not. She did not know how, but she too wondered at the mist's nature. It was an unseasonable fog, persisting in defiance of the summer sun, and its effect was to resist her return to the Citadel.

*Édan, Édan.*

She called to him silently, in that way they shared, but the wilderness of Samokea lay vast around her and he was yet too far away to hear.

The mist though, listened.

It rolled slowly, turning, drawing itself into the shape of a diaphanous woman adrift above the grass, her hair, her skin, her eyes, all distinguished only by subtle shadings of gray. She was one of the Inyomere that were the spirits of the Wild. And to Lanyon she said, "Why do you call to him? He does not want you to come."

Lanyon picked up her son and held him close, whispering to him, "Do not be afraid." Then she addressed the Inyomere, asking, "Did Édan send you to hinder me?"

The Inyomere of the mist drifted nearer, her hair billowing in wide, soft clouds. "I have heard his lamentations and the prayers he whispers in the night. He says, '*Do not let her come home to me. Do not let her come home. Better for her if she is lost in the Wild. Do not let her come home.*'"

Lanyon shook her head, astonished at such tidings and longing to reject them. Yet Inyomere knew only how to speak the truth. Never a lie from them. "Why would he speak thus? What does he intend?"

The mist drew back, bemused. Like most of her kin, it was not her way to ask why or what was to come. She was of the petty Inyomere: minor spirits of forest and meadow, stream and pool, the thickets, and the summer rain. Such concepts as time and purpose troubled only a few among the greater Inyomere.

The mist stooped lower, peering now at Lanyon's son. The little boy clung to his mother, as silent and still as a wild thing hiding in the grass, but his wide eyes did not turn away from the mist's soft gaze. She smiled at him. "When I look on him I remember his far mother, the Snow Chanter. His blood remembers her. She has given to him the will of the Inyomere."

"He is so much like his father," Lanyon whispered.

"Heed me, little sister. Do not go to Édan. He does not want you."

"That is something he must tell me himself, Blessed One. I beg you to relent. Unveil the sun and let us ride on."

"Come what may?" she asked softly.

Fear clutched at Lanyon's heart, but she agreed, "Come what may."

So the mist, in her rich voice, called for a wind to come, a breeze that hissed through the grass, and under its caress she turned and twisted, and slowly faded from Lanyon's sight.

Within minutes, the cloud-wrapped peaks of the Tiyat-kel stood revealed. Jahallon ordered the tents packed up again, and the company set out, this time with Siddél's rumbling thunder where it should be, on their right hand, as they made their way north.

Before long, they found the trail—a narrow track passing through meadow and grove on its way to the Citadel of the Snow Chanter—and for the rest of that day, they made good time. But Lanyon, who had not yet fully recovered from the birth, endured a long, wearying afternoon. And as she brooded over the words of the mist, her dread only grew.

At last Jahallon called a halt and the tents were set up again. The company knew to speak softly as they shared a simple meal of trail rations—unleavened nut bread, dried fish, and pemmican—while Lanyon mixed a cold gruel for her son.

She shared a tent with the other women, though she slept little, and when she did, the mist's warning continued to haunt her, re-echoing in her dreams: *He does not want you.*

At first light, one of the riders who had been on watch came through the camp, quietly waking the rest of the company. Lanyon arose, not eager for the day, but eager to be done with it. She sat cross-legged on a blanket, nursing her daughter in the predawn cold, while her sleepy-eyed boy huddled in Jahallon's lap, chewing on a biscuit. All around them, soft conversation, as the riders worked to stow the tents—still wet with the night's dew—and to saddle the horses.

"This will be another long day," Jahallon warned her. "I mean to reach the Citadel by evening."

Defying her misgivings, Lanyon assured him, "I am ready for it. I am ready to know the truth."

They set out before sunrise, under a clear sky, resting at intervals as the day passed. In the midafternoon, they came to a long valley, filled with green meadow grasses nodding at the touch of a light breeze. The baby in her carrier began to fuss, so Lanyon sang to her softly, hoping to comfort her. But she broke off her song at the sound of a distant cacophony of yips and wails. Raising her chin, she held her breath to listen.

The baby heard it too—the hue and cry of a hunting arowl pack. Even so young, she knew her peril, and began to mew in fear. Lanyon cradled her with an arm, whispering, "*Hush, hush.*"

Down the line came a command, passed quietly from rider to rider: "Make ready." Lanyon turned, relaying the order in turn, though it was not necessary. Those warriors behind her already held their bows with arrows nocked, preparing for yet another battle in the Long War that had been fought generation by generation, almost since the people first set foot on the Wild's southern shore.

No one went unarmed. Lanyon uncased her own bow, setting an arrow to the string as she resumed her quiet song, striving to offer what solace she could to her daughter while she watched the distant trees for any sign of movement.

Arowl were mad beasts, abominations, conjured into life by the wrathful magic of the Inyomere Siddél, made by him to prey on the people.

Siddél believed the people had come to the Wild by treachery, and that it was the will of the One who wakened the Inyomere that they should be destroyed or driven back into the sea. The Long War would not end until Siddél was made to leave the world, but he was one of the great Inyomere, and Lanyon did not know if that could even be.

The chorus of mad howls grew swiftly louder, overwhelming Lanyon's song. The baby gave voice to her terror with a plaintive wail, while Lanyon's mare pranced and snorted, a sheen of nervous sweat shining on her neck. From Jahallon, a sharp command that cut past the clamor, "Form up!" Warriors rode in from either end of the column to form defensive wings.

The baby's crying played hard against Lanyon's nerves. When the courier who was caring for her son brought him up beside her, Lanyon saw that he cried too, but silently.

"Courage, my love," she told him. He turned his little face away from her, hiding against the breast of his caretaker.

"There!" someone called. "Motion. In that line of trees."

Lanyon looked, and saw a shadow moving, but only for a moment before it withdrew. And after another moment, the arowl pack's low, bloodthirsty baying transformed into a chorus of high-pitched, fear-filled howls.

Sensing a new presence, Lanyon held her breath to listen. And low beneath the wailing pack, she heard a rumble of galloping hooves.

The warriors around her heard it too. Seven or eight youths, inspired by that sound, set heel to horse, lunging toward the trees. But Jahallon bellowed at them to stop and get back into line.

Bestial screeching erupted within the forest, panicked barking too, abruptly cut off. Very soon, the sound of hoofbeats faded, along with the last cries of the pack.

Lanyon shivered and put her bow away. Then she let her daughter nurse there in the saddle, to calm her as Jahallon ordered the company to move on.

They had gone another two miles or more, when Édan came. Lanyon reined in her mare to watch as he rode out of the forest with a hundred or more of his warriors around him, the tips of their spears bloody in the sunlight.

The Habaddon company cheered, calling out to their Samokeän allies in raucous greeting while Jahallon rode out to meet Édan. The two clasped hands and clapped shoulders, and Édan spoke for all to hear, "You have long been welcome in my home, Far Father. At last you have come."

Jahallon turned to look at Lanyon. "Go to her," he urged, his voice low but audible in a sudden lull of wind. "She has brought you a great gift."

Lanyon strove to steady herself, to present a calm face as Édan approached. She climbed down from the mare and took her daughter from the chest carrier, laying the baby against her shoulder and patting her gently.

Édan went first to his son and hugged him. "Ah, how you've grown."

The boy looked confused. It had been so long since he'd last seen his father, he did not truly remember. Édan handed him back to the woman who watched him. Then he slipped from the saddle and, leading his horse, he walked to meet Lanyon.

He looked more gaunt than she remembered, more careworn. Dressed in a simple tunic and trousers, worn boots, and a dark gray riding coat, there was nothing overt to distinguish him from any one of his men. Like them, he carried his sword on his back, and he kept his black hair confined in a heavy braid in the Samokeän way.

Lanyon had expected to see some cold expression on his comely face. Anger maybe, or contempt in his dark eyes. What she saw instead was a strange mingling of joy and grief. She wondered what it meant, and she wondered too at his silence.

But if he would not speak, then she must.

Holding the infant out to him, she said, "I have brought our daughter home."

Édan smiled and took her. The baby started to cry, but he spoke to her softly, soothingly, and she quieted. He kissed her forehead. Then he looked to Lanyon and said, "Let us go home."

Édan wanted her to ride with him on his horse. So she climbed up first, with the baby safe again in the carrier, and he sat behind her.

His people had not approved of their marriage. They mistrusted Lanyon's affinity with the Inyomere. A strange irony, given that all the Samokeäns were descended from one or another of the many children of the Inyomere Tayeraisa, who was called the Snow Chanter.

Long ago, when the people had first begun to explore the northern lands, Tayeraisa had met the warrior Samoket, the last of Jahallon's sons. Tayeraisa the Snow Chanter had been unique among the Inyomere. Curious and willful, it had pleased her to change herself to be as a woman of the people, and to take Samoket as her husband. Together they built the Citadel and brought forty-two children into the world before death finally took Samoket away—and from the hour of his passing the Snow Chanter was not seen again.

Among their descendants many shared somewhat in the magic of the Inyomere. So it was with Édan. He was the sorcerer-chieftain of Samokea, armed with a magic far greater than any Lanyon could command. And still his people complained *she* had too much of the Inyomere in her, and this was why the spirits sought her out when they scorned other people. Yet this affinity was the root of Édan's affection. It fascinated him that he could speak with her mind-to-mind, as the Inyomere spoke to one another. It was a connection that had captivated him from the first hour they met, when he was seventeen and she only eleven.

Many times Jahallon had warned her that such a fascination was no substitute for love, but at sixteen it had seemed enough. She seduced Édan and by the time Jahallon allowed them to marry she was three months pregnant. Now she was nineteen, and the time for making choices was long past.

For some time they rode in silence. Édan held her close, and the baby slept. But Lanyon could not pretend there was peace between them, and at last she asked what was foremost in her mind. "Were you so angry? That you hoped I would not come home?"

"I was never angry."

"No?" His denial provoked her temper. She quoted to him the words of the mist. "Do not let her come home to me. Better for her if she is lost in the Wild."

His breathing quickened. She felt the hammering of his heart. Finally, he said, "I would not have tried to stop you, if you had taken our children away south to the safety of Hallah."

"Édan!" She twisted around to face him, the baby protesting in soft bleats. "How could you think such a thing? That I would abandon the Long War and yield what my father and my brothers—*all* my family, and yours—have died to defend? If this is what you think of me—"

"Hush, hush." He kissed her at the corner of her mouth. "Say no more on it. I am chastened."

She turned away from him, facing forward again. Her lips brushed her daughter's warm, sweet-smelling scalp, a kiss of comfort for both of them. "Did you want me to take them away?"

He answered with a catch in his voice. "It was for you to decide."

"It was never a choice."

"Then you are braver than I am."

She heard grief in his voice. It made her fearful. Édan had grown up on the battlefield; he was not easily shaken. "Édan, what has happened to you? Was it this last campaign? Jahallon said it was hard-fought, that many of your warriors fell."

His arms tightened around her. "It was the last battle. It almost broke us. It was the worst I've ever seen. Worse than the winter your father and your brothers were killed."

"Tell me. I am not afraid."

He sighed. His voice grew softer. "We were at Nendaganon. We had come to the very rim of a great arowl pit and it came to us we should set it afire—set all the pits ablaze!—and put an end to Siddél's stronghold. But that was a mistake.

"The fire drove forth the half-formed arowl . . . thousands of them. Lanyon, they were horrible to look on, skinless, ravening, mad as are all their kind for the blood of the people, but with no fear of death. I could not instill any fear in them, or beguile them, or confuse them in any way. They refused to hear my voice and accepted no command.

"The beasts carried none of their usual weapons. They came armed with only teeth and claws. And still, two hundred twelve men were lost to them and it would have been more, but these arowl were flawed and unfinished. Their lives withered quickly. Those we did not slay soon died on their own."

She turned again to look at him, too stunned at first to speak. Then she whispered, "Jahallon said nothing of this horror. I did not know."

"He doesn't understand how strong you are."

"I'm sorry I wasn't there when you returned."

Again he kissed her. "I knew you would come home." He looked east, to the cloud-shrouded peaks of the Tiyat-kel where the taunting voice of Siddél rumbled in tired threat. "All that we do, you and I, we do for the good of the people, no matter the cost."

No matter the cost?

"Is there something you're not telling me? Some deeper meaning behind your words? Say it now, so I don't have to be afraid."

"No," he said softly, soothingly. "There's nothing more to say. We are born to war, but for this hour at least, let us be at peace."

*Homeland*

# 1

IN THE CITY of Habaddon, in the library of Jahallon, a young warrior of Clan Samoket lingered late into the night. A single oil lamp suspended on chains illuminated a book open to a page he had read many times before. He kept returning to it—this account of the long-ago night when disaster had befallen Samokea.

Jahallon-the-Undying had been present that night in the Citadel of the Snow Chanter, but even Jahallon had never unraveled the mystery of all that had happened, and why.

The manuscript told what was known, beginning with the banquet held that evening . . .

> . . . to celebrate the first visit of Jahallon to the Citadel of the Snow Chanter.
>
> As darkness fell, Siddél's thunder muttered and threatened, but the Samokeäns were accustomed to hearing the great Inyomere in his temper and it frightened them not at all. They went to their beds content, certain he would not dare to approach the city.
>
> But beyond all expectation, Siddél came.
>
> It was deep in the night when a great crash of thunder exploded above the Citadel. Jahallon sprang from his bed, to hear the mocking voice of the Inyomere Siddél shaking the stone walls. Long ago, Jahallon had wounded

Siddél with his spear and it was for this affront that Siddél cursed him, proclaiming that death should not have him no matter his wounds or his grief, and that his fate would be to witness all the horror of the people's downfall. But it was Jahallon who had ever after rallied the people in the Long War against Siddél, and on that night it was the same.

Jahallon seized his bow and went outside. There he heard the monster roar Édan's name, and these words: "I am come! To see you slain by your own spell."

Lightning struck the towers and the houses. Roofs burst into flame. The thunder was deafening and all was chaos as Jahallon went to seek Édan.

He came too late. The tower where the Chieftain kept his household was aflame. Even as Jahallon drew near, the roof collapsed and sparks rose up as if from a great chimney. So it was that Édan, Chieftain of Samokea, was slain by the Inyomere Siddél, and his wife and children with him.

A madness of fear descended on the people, but Jahallon spoke to them.

He commanded them to gather their children and their weapons even as the walls of the city collapsed beneath the hammer of Siddél's lightning. Many were crushed by falling stone or burnt to death by lightning fires. Many more were lost as a host of ravening arowl descended on the city, the were-beasts among them armed with spear and sword. But Jahallon would not let the Samokeäns despair. He arranged their retreat, leading them south to the Glycian River in a running battle against a numberless horde of arowl.

Fewer than half the Samokeäns who had gone to sleep in the Citadel that night lived to cross the Glycian River. It was learned later that no watch had been set that night. The walls were left unguarded. If there had been but one alert sentry with a bow, Siddél might have

been turned away.
   Yet it was not so.
   And Samokea was lost to the arowl.

One hundred thirty-seven years had passed since that time.

The young warrior who read this account was himself Samokeän—a far son of those who had survived that terrible retreat. His name was Bennek of Clan Samoket and though he was just fifteen he already had much skill and experience in the hunting of the blood-hungry arowl.

Bennek closed the book, wistful for what had been lost. His calloused fingers touched the pendant that gleamed at his throat. It had come to him from his mother, and from her mother's mother before that. Made of gold openwork, it depicted vines twined in a shallow triangle, with a flaming sun rising from the downward point. The pendant had been cast long ago in the smithies of the Citadel of the Snow Chanter, and it was the only thing he possessed that survived from that time. His weapons had been forged by his kin. His clothes—a tunic and trousers and soft, well-worn boots—he'd made himself from the heavy brown cloth woven in Habaddon and from leather he'd tanned.

He stood—a lean youth of fair height and not done growing yet. The oil lamp cast a warm glow across his bronze skin and gleamed in his smooth black hair. In allegiance to his Samokeän ancestors, Bennek wore his hair in the traditional braid down his back.

His alert gaze swept the room, confirming what he already knew: Once again, he was last to leave the library.

Handling the book carefully, Bennek returned it to its place on the shelf. Then he blew out the oil lamp and made his way into the starlit streets.

He'd come to Habaddon with his older brother and his cousin, both just seventeen. The three boys had been on their own for years, living in their family's keep in the forest of Fathalia, far from any other settlement. They might have been in Fathalia still, but over the winter a rare patrol out of Habaddon had brought news of a muster to be called by the Samokeän captains-in-exile who rode with Jahallon-the-Undying.

When spring came, the boys left behind all they knew, venturing to Habaddon to seek a place in the army—only to be disappointed in their hopes. The captains declared them too young and too unseasoned for battle. "Go home, grow in strength, and hone your skills." The army had ridden out without them, embarked on another of the endless campaigns of the Long War.

But the boys had not gone home. They had spent the summer in and around Habaddon, hunting at need and camping on the seashore or in the forest, coming into the city as often as it pleased them. In that time, Bennek had read every parchment and every book in the library and studied all the maps. Now with the approach of autumn, a sense of restlessness was waking in him.

He reached the city gate. The two women standing watch greeted him. The older of them asked, "Why do you and your kin sleep on the beach, Bennek? Do you not care for our city?"

He smiled. "Habaddon is a fine city, ma'am. But I am Samokeän, and since the fall of the Citadel, we have belonged to the Wild."

Her eyes narrowed. "*I* am Samokeän, yet I live within Habaddon's walls."

This claim startled Bennek. Nothing in her dress or bearing distinguished her from a woman of Habaddon. "Then it is your home," he said softly, and he went out into the night.

Bennek remembered asking his mother why they did not go to live in Habaddon. She had answered, "It's better to live in the Wild than to live by the charity of our Habaddon friends. You are Samokeän, Bennek. Never forget it! Never forget the homeland we have lost."

That was when she'd taken the pendant from her own neck and fastened it around his, though he'd been only eight years old. "To remind you," she explained.

Even as Bennek made his cautious way down the steep, lightless path to the cove, his thoughts returned to the mystery of that long-ago night when the Citadel of the Snow Witch had fallen.

Why had the Citadel's walls been left unguarded? What spell had the Chieftain Édan conjured that had consumed him?

Édan had been a great chieftain, more skilled in sorcery than any before him and beloved of his people and of Jahallon. Siddél's arowl could hardly stand against him, and in his day many believed the beasts would finally be eradicated from the Wild, and that the Long War would come to an end. Then came his last battle in Nendaganon, with its terrible loss of life. It was said that when Édan returned to the Citadel, he was not the same man.

Bennek looked across the cove toward the campsite hidden among the rocks. He could just make out the ruddy light of a fire gilding the face of a large boulder. A figure stood on top of the boulder. Bennek raised his hand in silent greeting and received a wave in return.

The ocean lay quiet, its waves no more than ripples, the dark water reflecting glints of starlight. Wood smoke suffused the still air, along with the delicious aroma of roasting fish. Bennek skirted the little fishing boats resting safely on the sand, then entered the shelter of the rocks.

The sardonic voice of his cousin, Kit, spoke softly from the darkness above his head, "Ah, Bennek, you are so late we thought you had finally found a girl to take you home and feed you."

"I have had such invitations," Bennek said in all seriousness as he came around a boulder into camp. "I have declined them though, since Marshal has said we must muster here each evening." He looked questioningly at his brother, who crouched in the sand, tending the fish filets that roasted over a bed of glowing coals. "Marshal, do you think I should accept, instead?"

Marshal wasn't much for humor, but for some reason a grin flashed across his face. "You would need to let us know."

Kit jumped down from the rock where he'd been standing, his brows drawn down in a scowl. "You have had invitations?"

The three had grown up together and looked much alike, as close kin will. All wore their hair in Samokeän braids and they spoke with a formality learned from their mothers. Marshal was more broad-shouldered than either Kit or Bennek, and had the start of a neat beard on his chin, while Kit had sharper features. And of course Bennek—being two years younger—suffered in height. It was his lot that for as long as he could remember, his brother and his cousin had both been at least a head taller than he.

Marshal and Kit had been born within days of one another. They were as close as twins and had never been apart. So although Marshal was soft-spoken and given to careful planning, while Kit was so often brash in word and deed, they seemed always to know what the other was thinking and they rarely disagreed.

Bennek had never shared in this easy harmony. For him, getting on with Kit took some care—and he felt sure the subject of girls would not gain him any peace. So he let it go. He had more exciting news.

"I saw a magic spell today," he told them.

All his life Bennek had heard tales of sorcery, but before today he had never seen a spell called—and neither had Marshal or Kit—so at once he had their full attention.

"It was spoken by a sage. She didn't realize I was there in the library. When she found out, she was angry. She did not want me to see it."

"Why not?" Marshal asked. "Was it wicked?"

"I don't know. It was a fire spell. She spoke it under her breath. I couldn't make out the words, but I felt a strange presence brush past me. Then one by one each oil lamp was set aflame."

"Was she Samokeän?" Kit asked.

Bennek nodded.

A talent for sorcery occurred only among the Samokeäns, who were the descendants of the Snow Chanter, but even with them it was rare—ever more so in the long years since the fall of Édan.

"She was very old," Bennek said. "The oldest person by far I have ever seen."

"Did you ask her about it?" Marshal wondered.

Bennek had a gift of far-seeing, and all of them suspected he might have a talent for spell-calling too, but they knew no spells. Until today, they had come across no one else who did.

"I tried to speak to her, but she didn't want to talk to me. She said if I was meant to know a spell like that, I would find it on my own. Then she left. I haven't seen her before in the library, and I think now she will make sure I don't see her again."

Bennek and Kit went to sleep beside the campfire while Marshal stood watch. It was their custom for Marshal to take the first watch, Kit to stand guard in the middle night, and Bennek to keep the last watch before dawn.

So out of habit Bennek awakened as soon as Kit touched his shoulder. The fire had gone out, and the only light came from the stars.

Taking his spear, Bennek walked a little away from the camp, climbing atop a boulder so that he could get a good view of the cove and the curve of the beach. Nothing stirred except the gentle waves, until the sky began to lighten in the cold blue hour before sunrise. Then an owl soared out over the water. Bennek watched it circle around and fly inland again—straight at him.

He had been leaning on his spear. But as the owl approached, he gripped the spear in two hands. If he had to, if the bird did not veer away, he would use the shaft to fend it off.

But just before the owl reached him, it spread its wings, hovering a moment before gracefully alighting on a pedestal of rock, so close he heard the scratch of its claws even over the sighing of waves against the beach.

Bennek lowered his spear and bowed in respect, knowing this was no owl but a spirit that took that form, one of the Inyomere of the Wild.

In an eye-blink, the owl's gray shape dissolved, becoming a small girl. She crouched on the rock, dressed in a gown of feathers, with a feather circlet to tame her long hair. The light of lingering stars glittered in her wide eyes as she peered at him, unblinking. When she spoke, it was in a whispery, scolding voice. "Bennek, how long will you tarry here when the wicked arowl still howl in your homeland? Come forth to the hunt before Siddél's mad beasts devour all the Wild!"

Then the Inyomere became an owl again and leapt away into

the air, soaring up from the cove, rising past Habaddon's strong walls. A sentry on the northern wall stopped her pace to watch the owl's flight. All else remained still. Even the prayer ribbons that usually snapped and fluttered above the walls hung limp on their poles in the quiet air.

Yet Bennek was aquiver. He turned and jumped down from the boulder where he'd kept watch, calling out, "Marshal! Marshal, you must waken! Kit, you must not laugh when I tell you what has befallen us."

Marshal appeared, spear in hand. "What report?" he whispered. Kit loomed like a shadow behind him.

"It is no danger," Bennek assured them. He glanced at the path that descended to the cove. Very soon the fishers would come that way to start another day upon the water, but they had not yet left the city gate. "An Inyomere came to me just now. She spoke to me."

It was common enough to see the spirits, but seldom did they speak, and never before had any addressed Bennek by name. Wonder tinged his voice as he told them of the owl. Yet his story did not rouse in them the joy he'd expected.

Kit turned to Marshal. "It is just the same!" he said in bitterness.

"The same?" Bennek asked. "The same as what?"

The rising light picked out a troubled look on Marshal's face. "The very same words we heard last night. This owlish Inyomere came to me at first watch, and then in the middle night she came to Kit."

"Kit did not say this when he wakened me—he said nothing!—yet you told it to one another?"

"Do not be angry." Marshal touched his forehead. "Your sight is deepest, and we only hoped you would hear something different."

"I have heard that we should seek our homeland, and this seems good to me! Marshal, we have been in Habaddon for all this summer. I have read all there is to read in the library and seen all the maps. What is left for us to do? I would have been happy to serve as a warrior in Jahallon's army, but we were not allowed to do that and the army is long gone away without us. What reason is left for us to stay?"

Neither Kit nor Marshal had any good answer.

"There is nothing for us here," Bennek insisted against his brother's silence. "Let us be away. Marshal? You can't mean to refuse the challenge of this owlish Inyomere."

Marshal turned back to the cold ashes of the fire. "Bennek, it's not in my heart to return to Fathalia. Not so soon as this."

It was true they did not have much to go home to. Their warrior fathers had long ago fallen to the arowl, leaving their mothers to raise them together in the family keep. Their mothers had been as fierce as any warriors of Clan Samoket, teaching their sons forestcraft, hunting, reading, writing, and weaponry, but in time they too perished, brought down by a pack of ravening arowl.

In the seven years since, the boys had lived mostly by their own will and wits, and much of that time had been spent hunting the wicked arowl so that the forest of Fathalia remained a wholesome place and the Inyomere there were happy and often seen. But the boys dreamed of greater deeds.

In bitterness Kit said, "I would not go back to Fathalia though all the Inyomere of the Wild command it."

Bennek shook his head in puzzled disbelief. "I do not understand you. The owl did not bid us to return to Fathalia. That is only where we were born. It is not our homeland."

Kit looked at him with sharp eyes, but Marshal laughed in a contented way. He turned to Kit. "It is as I said. Bennek has heard it differently."

"We are to go to Samokea," Kit said in astonishment. Still, he could hardly believe it. He wanted to be sure. "We are agreed? That is the meaning?"

"It is clear," Bennek insisted. "We are called to it."

Marshal nodded, and though his eyes were merry, he spoke in a whisper as if they were on a hunt. "Jahallon's captains would not have us, but this is a better thing—to give our service to the land that was once the home of our people."

He glanced toward the bluff, where the early light had begun to pick out the texture of Habaddon's strong walls. On the path, the first of the fisher folk could be seen, making their way down to the cove.

"Let us not speak it aloud again. The good people of Habaddon might make issue of our going."

Kit was content. "Ah Bennek, you require much looking after, but how shall I complain of it when you unravel such mysteries for us?"

"Your complaints are swift enough if I do not find arowl for you to hunt."

Kit laughed—he could not deny it—but Marshal said, "Peace, men. Remember where we are bound, and let us be as one."

# 2

In Habaddon the women fished and farmed and kept the watch, and some among them hunted, but it was not their way to wander far from the walls, so meat was a rarity when the men were away to war. As a consequence, the hunting skills of the Samokeän boys had been much in demand, and several times they had brought back small forest deer, and once an elk calf.

Their efforts were not forgotten. When they went around the city to make their farewells they were gifted with dried beef and venison, raisins, flatbread, roasted nuts and smoked fish. When asked where they were going, Marshal explained, "We are bound for our homeland, and will not return for some long time." All who heard this assumed they meant to return to Fathalia.

The young woman who now stood watch at the gate wished them good fortune, "For the Wild is fickle and treacherous, and the Inyomere who keep it do not love us."

"Ah, but they love the arowl less," Kit replied, "and at the least we are well-armed."

Each carried a spear, a sword, a bow, and a quiver with many arrows. They also had a store of steel arrowheads, for though they could make arrowheads of stone, the steel heads were larger and more deadly.

It was not yet noon when they set off down the wide path that led to the wheat fields and from there to the forest beyond. They had just started across the first field when they heard the sound of a wind rushing up the coast from the south.

Bennek turned, looking up as the swift breeze caught the streamers of the prayer ribbons that flew from poles on Habaddon's high wall. Red and yellow, bright blue, and lively green, the leather banners coiled and snapped, and as the wind swept past them it carried away with it the prayers that had been stamped on them, each a tiny charm for the renewal of the Wild.

"The south wind blesses the way for us," Kit said.

Marshal nodded. "Let us follow as swiftly as we may."

They kept to the track the men of Habaddon used to reach the Glycian River, which marked the northern boundary of the Protected Lands—that territory under Jahallon's watch. On the northern side of the Glycian lay lost Samokea.

The men of Habaddon had long ago made it their duty to keep watch along the river. Even in the season of war, enough remained in Habaddon to patrol the riverbank, hunting for any sign of arowl that had dared to cross over from Samokea. They allowed no such beast to survive. But the patrols did not keep watch against young warriors venturing north into Samokea. Why should they? None had ever dared such a venture before.

Still, Marshal believed there would be trouble if they encountered a patrol. The men would surely object if they knew what the Samokeän boys intended. So after walking north for several hours, the boys left the track and, angling east, they went on in stealth through the woods. The south wind befriended them in this, for it hissed through the forest, filling it with sound and the motion of swaying branches, disguising their passage with its play.

That night they camped without a fire, and by mid-morning on the following day they reached the Glycian's slow, winding waters.

Bennek gazed at the river with misgiving. "It's so much wider here than in Fathalia."

They stood just within the cover of the trees, looking out across the gray water. The northern bank seemed but a reflection of the south. On both sides of the river the wind shook the trees and tossed their branches. White flecks skipped across the water.

"The river protects Habaddon," Marshal said. "The arowl fear the water, and they are weighted by their weapons, so they will only cross at dire need."

From his pack Kit fetched a small hand ax. "We at least will have a raft to float our gear. Bennek, if you grow tired during our swim, you may cling to it and rest."

In a flash of pique, Bennek answered, "You are all kindness, my cousin, but your need might be greater. I have swum the Glycian before."

That had been the day his mother and Kit's had been taken by the arowl. Bennek had been with them, but he'd escaped because they held off the beasts long enough for him to dive into the flooding river's wild current. For years, Bennek had refused to speak of that day. He wished he'd held onto his silence because now Kit was staring at him with a shocked expression, while Marshal asked in concern, "You are remembering that day?"

Bennek did not require such coddling. "Why do you look at me so?" he demanded. "I am not sad. I think on it sometimes, but that day is not like this. We are bound for Samokea! And the south wind prepares the way."

Indeed, it blew hard all day as they gathered fallen logs. It roared through the forest, causing even the great trees to bend and groan. The rap of Kit's ax as he smoothed and shaped the logs was lost in the tumult, while everywhere green leaves swirled through the air.

Late in the day they set to binding the logs together with cording, securing them with cross-braces laid in the notches Kit had made. To ensure their gear stayed well above the water, they added a second layer of large sticks.

The last rays of sunset reached up the river, limning them in its glow as they tested the raft in a quiet eddy.

"It's beautiful," Bennek said, standing in the water beside it. "The wood is dry and floats well."

"Climb on it," Marshal urged. So Bennek did, and the raft sank only a little. Marshal smiled in satisfaction. "We've done well, men. Let's rest awhile now and eat. When full darkness has fallen, we'll cross."

They drew the raft out of the water, though it required much effort. For the second evening they made no fire, but ate dried rations in the gathering dark.

"How close are the arowl, Bennek?" Kit asked after a time. "I've heard no howl all this day."

"They are not far."

Bennek gazed into the twilight shadows across the river. He could see nothing there but the shapes of trees rising up to brush the early stars. Nor could he hear any howl or moan or other lamentation of the arowl, and as for their foul scent, that was swept away by the south wind. But though darkness and distance hid the beasts, Bennek still had means to find them.

It was his gift that he could send his awareness wandering forth. Whenever he did this, it seemed to him he became a ghost, for he left his body behind him. The trance that let him enter the spirit-world came easily, so while Kit and Marshal waited, he closed his eyes and slipped away from himself—an unencumbered ghost gliding swiftly over the water and on into the trees.

Many seconds later he returned, shaking his head to clear the dizziness and disorientation that always followed a visit to the spirit-world.

"There's a small pack of four arowl," he reported. "Maybe half a mile beyond the river. They've been there much of the day, but they're restless now, because another pack has bedded down not a mile to the east."

This news drew a grim chuckle from Kit. "Our luck holds. Let them hunt one another! Then there will be only the fiercest, the cleverest left for us to take."

Marshal stood up. Stars had taken over the sky. "It's time."

They stripped to bare skin, making bundles of their clothes. Bennek rubbed mud on his pendant so it wouldn't glimmer in the starlight. They hauled the raft into the eddy of calm water, then secured their weapons to it, along with their clothes, and their packs. The water was cold, but the wind on their wet skin was bone-chilling.

"Quietly," Marshal said, "but with all haste."

They pushed the raft until the water became so deep they had no choice but to swim, clinging with cold fingers to the wood. Then the current took hold, sweeping them downriver. That was no surprise, but they had not guessed the wind would also seize the raft, turning it round and round so that if they kicked they were as likely to propel it back toward the southern shore as to hurry its passage to Samokea.

But it was the will of the wind that they should cross. Slowly, slowly, its great breath drove them toward the northern bank. The black shadow of the trees loomed ever taller, and finally Marshal whispered, "We are across! There is mud beneath my feet. Push! Push to the shore!"

It took Bennek some time longer before he could touch bottom, but when he was able, he braced himself against the sucking mud and, using all his lean muscles, he helped Kit and Marshal to push the raft into the shallows.

They found no welcoming eddy. The current fought them as they struggled to ground the raft, but finally they succeeded in hauling it out onto a narrow mud beach. Water burbled past its corners. A few steps away a dark embankment rose up higher than their heads. They hurried to untie their clothes and weapons, dressing quickly, and then strapping on their swords.

The horsemen of Habaddon carried heavier weapons, but hunting on foot, the boys preferred a light sword with a thin curved blade. This they carried in back scabbards so as not to catch in brush or thick grass. The hilt stood up above the shoulder and the curve of the blade aided the speed of their draw.

Bennek shrugged a bow case over the same shoulder, with a quiver of arrows attached.

No words had yet been spoken.

Marshal tapped Bennek to get his attention. Then, palm down, he rotated his hand. *Look around.*

Bennek first flipped up the collar of his coat against the wind.

Then he found a dry stone and, easing his weapons aside, he sat down. Closing his eyes, he slipped away once more into the night.

Marshal and Kit set to untying the cording that bound the raft together. This they kept, while the logs were left on the beach for the current to take at its whim.

After a few minutes, Bennek stirred. He said, "It's safe to speak. There are no arowl near us. We've come far down the river, and will have to go back some distance before we can hunt."

As Bennek stood, Marshal handed him his pack. It was a simple sack with a single strap that looped across his chest. His spear was strapped to it, the shaft broken down into two parts and protected in a sheath.

"We're not going back," Marshal told him. "There are arowl all up and down the river. If we leave corpses for them to find, it will be only a few hours before we become the hunted. We'll go north instead. Quietly."

Bennek did not hide his outrage. "We can't leave these arowl unchallenged! Marshal, that's not our way."

"We're in Samokea now," Kit reminded him. "It's a place and time for new strategies."

"Come," Marshal said. "I want to look about."

They climbed the embankment, but saw only darkness beneath the wind-tossed trees.

Marshal signaled for them to be still. Seconds passed. Then he said, "Listen. Do you hear it? It's the faintest of voices . . . yet not lost to the wind."

"I do hear it," Kit said. "Surely that's an Inyomere?" He leaned forward, listening. Then he stopped up his ears. "I hear her still! She speaks to our hearts. She calls us to her."

Bennek heard nothing—not at first—not until he set aside his own disgruntled thoughts. Then he sensed it too—a prayer from the north, an appeal to the people of Samokea to come home, come home . . .

Even in his excitement, Bennek did not let his voice grow loud. "Marshal, that is the Snow Chanter! She lives! She calls to us!"

"Bennek, you are sure?"

"*Yes*," he breathed, overcome with awe, for the Snow Chanter was the mother of Samokea.

"I don't know how it could be," Marshal said in quiet astonishment. "Tayeraisa the Snow Chanter has not been seen in the world since the death of Samoket. Yet my own heart says it is her."

"As does mine," Kit agreed, wonder in his voice. Then he added in a reverent tone, "Surely this is the reason the owlish Inyomere summoned us. That we might cross the river and hear the lament of our far mother."

"It must be so," Marshal said. "And we must find her. It feels to me as if she suffers, and that she is calling us to help her in her need. Bennek, isn't it so?"

"Yes, and of course we must go." To know the Snow Chanter still existed within the Wild was a blessing; to be called to her service was the highest honor.

They set out at once—slowly at first, since only a little starlight reached beneath the trees to show the way. But within an hour they came to a rolling land with lightly forested hills to either side and between them a wide expanse of waist-high grass that glimmered beneath a sky resplendent with stars.

They moved swiftly after that, though every mile or so Marshal would call a brief halt, a chance for Bennek to search for nearby arowl.

The beasts were not of the Wild, so they stood apart from it and were easy for Bennek to perceive. Even behind hills, or among thickets, or crouched within the night's shadows—if they were present at all—his gaze would be drawn by their dark illumination. But on that night Bennek discovered no more arowl than the two small packs he had seen before, and both remained at rest, far to the east.

He wondered if chance had emptied the land of arowl, or if it was the will of the Snow Chanter that the way north should be open to them. Once, she had been a power among the Inyomere. It was said that when summer storms raged around the Citadel, she would stand atop the walls and chant a summons, calling the snow down from the mountain peaks to cool the thunderous temper of Siddél. But on this night her voice, weak when it first reached them, soon faded into silence.

This did not discourage the boys. Instead, it made their task feel more urgent. Putting weariness aside, they pressed on until the gleam of dawn filled the thickets with bird song. Then they climbed a rocky height from which they could look out on the surrounding land, and they made a camp.

All were tired, but they were pleased, too. Kit said, "Surely we are as deep into Samokea as anyone has been since the fall of our Chieftain Édan."

"And yet we have not slain a single arowl," Bennek grumbled, as he made a bed for himself beneath a thicket, cushioned by fallen leaves. "It's intolerable that we should pass through Samokea unchallenged."

"Be patient," Kit chided him. "Now that daylight has come, the arowl will stir. With luck they will find our trail."

Marshal frowned. "Has it now become a sign of luck to be hunted by the arowl?"

"Truly, my cousin," Kit answered him. "And we may soon find ourselves the luckiest of men."

But it was not to be.

"Bleak news," Kit said when he wakened Bennek in late morning. "No arowl pack has yet come howling down our trail."

Bennek stretched and groaned. "Do not think less of me, but I am pleased to hear it." He crawled out from beneath the thicket where he had gone to sleep, brushing the leaf litter from his hair and shaking it from his blanket. "Kit, I have dreamed of snow and ice at the top of high mountains. My heart is filled with the wordless prayers of the Snow Chanter. She is trapped somewhere, and in dire need. I confess I am eager to go to her."

Kit shook out his own blanket as he prepared to go back to sleep. Since he kept the middle watch, his rest was always divided in two parts. "The Snow Chanter spoke to me too as I slept. The mountains she shows us must be the Tiyat-kel. That is her home, and she is an Inyomere who is bound to her place."

Bennek nodded. On the maps in Jahallon's library, the Tiyat-kel were shown as a chain of high peaks, arising in southern Samokea and marching north, beyond all knowledge. To the west of the mountains lay the lost iron quarries of the Armory Peaks, and the ruins of the Citadel of the Snow Chanter. In the east, where they now wandered, there had been no settlements.

Later, when Marshal woke, he described the same dreams. "Let's go on, this very afternoon. It's warm today, but autumn is nigh and the high peaks will soon be encumbered with snow. We have no time to waste."

They set out in the pleasant sunshine of middle-afternoon. Now and then Bennek searched the land with his spirit sight, but the arowl remained far away. They camped at dusk, setting out again at sunrise, and that day was much the same as the last.

On the third day though, gray clouds filled the sky, and their fortune changed. At mid-morning, Bennek sensed an arowl pack some miles to the south. "The beasts have found our trail. It's a large pack, seventeen in number, and they run swiftly."

Marshal, ever cautious and careful, continuously studied the lands through which they passed, marking in his mind the distance to each hill, how it could best be climbed, and where a defense might be made. So Bennek's news did not fluster him. "We'll prepare our own hunt," he said. "There, on that hill to the west. It's not half a mile away."

The hill had height enough to provide a good view of the land around, but it was not Marshal's plan to climb to the stony summit. Instead, he meant to make use of the steep slopes clothed in thickets and hardy trees. He positioned himself and Kit near the base, a bow-shot apart, but he sent Bennek higher. "There you'll have an overview, and while you're entranced you'll be safe from the first assault."

So Bennek climbed alone up through the thickets, halfway to the crown. From that height he saw a river glimmering in the east. His study of maps told him it must be the River Talahnon that ran east and then south out of the Tiyat-kel. They planned to meet that river and follow it for a time.

The first faint howls of the arowl pack reached him on the wind. He turned to look out over the grasslands to the south, smiling in anticipation.

# 3

Marshal crouched within the thickets, listening to the crying and howls of the pack as it drew steadily closer. Seventeen arowl. Never had they faced such numbers. In Fathalia, the largest pack they'd ever hunted had numbered only nine beasts. Still, they were well prepared—and what was the point of doubt?

The first arowl ambled around the shoulder of a grassy rise not an eighth of a mile away. Marshal saw it and sucked in a sharp breath. He'd heard stories of arowl like this, but never before had he seen one.

Arowl had many shapes and habits, but those that stood on two legs and possessed other features of the people were called were-beasts. Were-wolves were most common. Marshal had met several in Fathalia, though most of the arowl there went on four feet and weighed no more than a man.

What he saw now was a towering were-bear, easily seven feet in height. Though it walked upright with a man's square shoulders and rolling gait, it had the head of a beast, furred, with ears at the top of its skull and a long, scarred snout. But even at such a distance Marshal could see the whites of its eyes.

Siddél had made his were-beasts with the eyes of the people because it disturbed the warriors who fought against them; and he had given them weapons like those the people used. This wear-bear carried a sword hanging from a belt at its gray and scabrous belly, and it clutched a bow in its thick hands. Scraggly dull black fur covered it everywhere except on its belly and its lower chest, where rib bones appeared poised to cut right through its foul skin. Hunger made a man weak, but hunger drove the arowl to madness. The fiercest beast was the one closest to death.

As Marshal watched, the were-bear raised its snout to sniff at the air. It uttered an eerie low wail, answered at once by a second giant wear-bear that came loping around the low hill.

Marshal shivered. The impending battle had just gotten far more dangerous.

The two beasts stood together, snarling and barking at one another as if conversing on strategy, while around them the tall grass thrashed with the passage of other arowl, running so low to the ground Marshal could not yet see them.

Behind these came six agile, cat-like arowl, yammering as they bounded on long, thin legs. Were-wolves ran with them, but Marshal couldn't get a good count because they kept ducking below the grass to run faster on all four legs.

Seventeen arowl.

His heart beat hard and fast.

Arowl could be convinced to retreat, but they would always return to the hunt. Though they would eat whatever poor creature they could seize, their only purpose and pleasure was to consume the flesh of the people—a desperate craving that ensured this battle would not be ended until all seventeen lay dead.

Drawing a deep breath to steady himself, he readied his bow.

Hidden within a thicket, Bennek closed his eyes and summoned the trance that let him slip into the spirit world. His will became a vapor, streaming out to meet the ravening pack. As he curled around them and between them he felt their unquenchable fury and their endless hunger.

The howling beasts went into a frenzy when they reached the foot of the hill and discovered the many scent trails Kit and Marshal had left for them. Knowing their prey to be nearby, none wanted to come late to the feast. In an eye blink, the structure of the pack collapsed, the arowl scattered, and each began to hunt only for itself.

*Thwak!*

A bow sounded from Marshal's position, and a moment later, from Kit's.

One of the huge were-bears fell with an arrow in its eye. A few steps away, a four-footed beast like a giant weasel staggered and collapsed.

Arowl were not mindless. They understood the trajectory of an arrow. The pack re-formed in two parts as the beasts bore down on each archer.

Bennek used that moment to strike at them from within the spirit world. He breathed out a miasma of fear for the beasts to breathe in. The effect was stunning to see. The arowl were confounded. They lost their reason, and all sense of purpose. Some turned and fled into the grass, but most plunged into the thickets to hide themselves, while more arrows flew, bringing down one, and another, and another still. Bennek reached out again with his will and caused two of the cat-like beasts to fall upon one another.

This ability to confound the arowl had come to Bennek from his Samokeän forebears. The Chieftain Édan was known to have set fear in the minds of whole hosts of beasts. Bennek contended with lesser numbers, but he was well-practiced. Only by his skill had he and Marshal and Kit been able to hunt the arowl packs out of Fathalia.

But now some of the panicked beasts fled up the hill, directly toward his position.

"Bennek!" Marshal shouted. "Wake up! Wake up now!"

Recognizing his peril, Bennek returned to himself just as something came crashing through the thickets below him. Something big.

Swaying, still dizzy from his venture into the spirit world, he grabbed his bow. Scrambling to his knees, he fitted an arrow to the bowstring, then looked down to see the second were-bear bounding upslope, sword in hand.

Its face resembled the face of a bear, but corrupted, as if its skull had grown all wrong: the snout too short, the face too flat, and its forehead heavy with knobs and swellings. Some recent brawl had left its ears torn down to bloody scraps. But its eyes were sharp and bright, with whites like the eyes of the people.

The were-bear caught sight of him kneeling within the thicket. It bounded toward him, snout furrowed in a hideous snarl, revealing fangs fully two inches long and gleaming white.

Bennek did not flinch. He wanted to make this kill himself. He wanted it for his mother. For Kit's mother. But he had to act fast, before Kit and Marshal shot it first. So he drew his bow while still on his knees and let the arrow fly.

It struck the beast between the eyes and stuck there—but the were-bear kept coming.

Bennek scrambled out of the thicket so he would not be hindered in his second shot. As the wear-bear closed on him, its sword raised for a killing stroke, he fired a second arrow. It struck the beast in its left eye. The arowl's head snapped back; it spun, and this time, it fell.

Before it hit the ground, Bennek nocked another arrow. The sound of twigs crackling in the thicket where he had just been told him something else was coming. He saw dry leaves scattering in the air and then a glimpse of a weasel-beast. He bent his bow, released the arrow. It struck the beast in its black nose, biting deep. The thing screeched, tossing its head up and down as it struggled to shake the arrow loose until, abruptly, it collapsed.

From the corner of his eye, Bennek saw another of the same kind racing toward him up the slope. He turned, but before he could shoot, two arrows from below brought it down.

Those arowl that had fled to the safety of the grass yammered in fear, but on the hill a hush had fallen.

"Bennek!" Marshal called. "Your count?"

"Only two." He consoled himself with the presence of the surviving arowl, waiting in the grass.

"I have four," Kit called, "counting the one we felled together."

"I have four not counting it," Marshal answered, "leaving seven still in the grass."

Quickly, Bennek slipped his bow into its case. Then he pulled his spear from the sheath on the side of his pack, knowing Marshal would next order a pursuit. It took but a moment to twist an extension onto the spear's shaft.

A howl of agony broke out behind him.

Bennek whirled around, astonished that an arowl had gained the high ground. Surprise became shock when he saw a were-wolf looming above him, only a little more than a stone's throw away. Exactly like a man it looked in body—it was even clothed in a tunic and belt—but its head was fey wolf, with reddened eyes that rolled back in its skull as it howled again in dire pain, for it was on fire.

The wolf's chest burned with a searing white flame. A smaller were-wolf—also on fire—leaped past it, running on all fours, howling and snapping and setting the hillside ablaze. Higher still on the slope, Bennek saw a black shape drop down from a gnarled persimmon tree and scuttle away.

All this he glimpsed in a moment.

Then the tall wolf, maddened with pain and panic, leaped downhill, tumbling and getting up again, igniting the thickets while the blazing fire spread to consume all its body. In its blind death agony it plunged straight toward Bennek.

He dropped the spear and seized his bow again. Frantically he nocked an arrow and shot at the wolf's chest, aiming at the densest flame. The wolf toppled, senseless, a burning mass that came to rest just five paces from him.

"Hallo!" Kit called. "Bennek has learned the fire trick after all."

"It wasn't me!"

Kit stood in the open, gazing up with his bow drawn.

"I glimpsed a thing lurking higher on the hillside," Bennek told him.

Marshal came crashing up through the thickets, following the path made by the slain were-bear, his face flushed and his spear ready. "Are you wounded?"

"No!"

"Then what did you see?"

"Two wolves ablaze, and a small black figure dropping from a tree . . . just there." He pointed. "I couldn't tell what it was, but it has an Inyomere's magic."

Marshal nodded. Then he turned to look downhill. Terror had won out over hunger, and the remaining arowl were fleeing, racing away through the grass toward the distant sheen of the River Talahnon. "Kit! Retrieve what arrows you can. Bennek and I will discover what lurks above."

Kit grinned. "I'll meet you at the top. Bennek, do not let the flames box you in!"

Bennek turned an uneasy gaze on the burning thickets.

"It's spreading, but not quickly," Marshal assured him. So they went first to retrieve arrows from the fallen arowl on the slope. When they had found all, Bennek paused to look once more at the retreating arowl. He counted five survivors, already tiny with distance.

"Do you think they will find more of their kind?" he asked Marshal.

"Probably, but we'll take them however many they are. Come. Let's get around these flames before Kit beats us to the top of the hill."

Kit caught up with them as they explored the ground around the ancient persimmon tree. Close to the trunk, Marshal found scuffed tracks that looked to have been made by small, thin-soled shoes. "It has to be one of the Inyomere," he said in a low, cautious voice. "I have heard of no one among the people who can command such a fire spell. Not in our time."

"Though our Chieftain Édan was said to have this skill," Bennek mused. And if Édan could call such a spell, might he learn to do it too?

"Look there!" Kit breathed in an urgent whisper.

Bennek turned to find his cousin gazing up at an outcropping of white rock on the hilltop.

"I saw it there in the rocks," Kit said. "Watching us, I expect."

Marshal looked at Bennek. "Put your spear away. We must meet this Inyomere in peace, or not at all."

Petty Inyomere existed everywhere in the Wild. Most were simple creatures, their magic subtle, slow, and earthy. But powerful spirits could be encountered too—strong winds, great rivers, deep winter snow—and these were easily offended.

So Bennek did as Marshal said, and stowed his spear. Then they continued to climb, the fire following after them, moving gradually up the hill.

They stopped just below the rocks. The Inyomere had hidden itself, but Marshal called to it anyway, "Greetings, Blessed One! We are three warriors come home to Samokea. We hunt the arowl but have no quarrel with any spirit save the monster Siddél. Will you let us pass?"

Many seconds slipped by. Bennek felt sure the Inyomere would not show itself. But then a stir of motion drew his gaze—and his heartbeat quickened.

A figure, hooded and robed in black, stepped cautiously from behind a giant block of white stone. The wind caught the hem of its garment, sending it billowing over black leggings, but crisscrossed straps held the robe in place over its chest . . . or over her chest. She had a woman's figure, and when she pushed her hood back she revealed a face like that of a woman of the people. Her coppery hair danced on the wind in long, loose strands, lashing around two small bundles that she carried, one on her back, and one at her side. She appeared lithe and young, but that meant nothing, for the Inyomere were as old as the Wild. She looked them over with a wary, doubtful gaze, but said nothing.

Marshal spoke again. "We thank you for striking down the two were-wolves that came behind us. The battle would have been close if they had lived to fight."

Bennek watched her closely, expecting her to disappear or become something other. But she stayed, and to his amazement she answered Marshal with polite words, though she had a strange lilt to her voice. "No thanks are needed, good sir. The arowl are the enemy of all the people."

"The arowl are also the enemy of those Inyomere who have foresworn the blasphemy of Siddél," Marshal said.

Her eyes narrowed in annoyance. "Sir, do you know of any such?"

Marshal glanced urgently at Kit, but the only advice he received was a shrug. "I meant you, Blessed One."

"Good sir, you mistake me! I am no Inyomere. I am one among the people."

Could it be true? Bennek stepped forward, eyes narrowed in suspicion. "What you did to the arowl—surely that is an Inyomere's magic?"

"Please. I am no Inyomere."

"Yes, ma'am," Marshal said. "Forgive us." He gave Bennek a dark look for speaking out of turn.

"Sirs, the fire is spreading. Perhaps you should come away."

Indeed, the flames were crackling slowly through the thickets toward their position.

"May we approach you then?" Marshal asked eagerly. "We could speak further and share some news of this land."

She turned an anxious gaze toward the flames. "If you will, if it pleases you—just come away before the fire draws near."

They scrambled around the shoulder of the hill while the woman made her way down from the rocks. She met them in the leafy shade of a chestnut tree just turning to its autumn foliage. The boys bowed to her and she returned this courtesy, though she looked at them with caution in her eyes.

Bennek studied her in turn, full of curiosity. He had seen no woman like her before. In Habaddon the women tended to be tall, with a graceful strength. By contrast, she was slight and very thin, with hollow cheeks, and knobby bones showing at her wrists. Her hair was a shade of copper he had only ever seen in paintings hanging in Jahallon's keep. Her black robe, though new and well-made, was much too large for her, causing Bennek to wonder why she would labor over such a fine garment, yet not make it to fit. Of the two straps that crossed her chest, one held a rectangular bag like a warrior's field kit; tied to the bag were a blanket and flask. The other strap held a long, thin bundle against her back. Bennek eyed it, but it was wrapped in gray cloth and he could not tell what it contained.

He noticed something else then, something that could not be seen but only sensed: the presence of wickedness. He looked around the shady hollow, suspicious that a true Inyomere lurked somewhere near. Or perhaps it was an unkind ghost.

Marshal, though, appeared untroubled—and this struck Bennek as peculiar, for usually his brother noticed first when an Inyomere was about. But he showed no concern beyond making a proper introduction: "Greetings, ma'am. I am Marshal of Clan Samoket. This is my brother Bennek, and our cousin, Kit."

"Well met, good sirs. I'm Lanyon Kyramanthes."

Bennek startled at this claim. In Habaddon, he had read about Clan Kyramanthes. They were the first clan, older by far than Clan Samoket. Known as the people of the tents, they had liked to move from one place to another in their homeland of Ohtangia, retreating to their fortresses only when arowl came ravaging through their lands. But Kyramanthes had been lost to war and tragedy long ago.

"How can you be of Kyramanthes?" Bennek wanted to know. "That clan is said to be long extinguished."

Kit snorted, and Marshal gave him a pained look. Bennek answered with a scowl because it *was* a valid question.

Marshal said, "Forgive him, Lanyon Kyramanthes. He is young."

"So are you all! Are you yet seventeen, sir?"

"I am, and Kit as well. Bennek is fifteen this past summer."

Bennek remained all too aware of the nearness of some wicked thing. Wanting to find it before it threatened them, he edged away, looking in the grass and in the low branches of the tree while keeping half an eye on Lanyon.

"How is it you are in Samokea?" she asked Marshal. "Surely you are not alone here? Did you come with your fathers?"

"Our fathers are dead, Lanyon, slain in battle long ago. We are in Samokea on our own."

Bennek, who had circled around to Lanyon's side, turned to Marshal with an expectant look. Surely he would not keep their purpose secret? Marshal met his gaze, and nodded silent assent.

"We have been called here by Tayeraisa the Snow Chanter, blessed mother of Clan Samoket."

Lanyon had an open face. She looked from Marshal to Bennek and back again, her astonishment and uncertainty plain to see. "Surely the Snow Chanter was lost to the Wild long ago?"

Kit answered her. "She has wakened." He told of the owlish Inyomere that had chastised them. "So we set out for our homeland, and on the night we crossed the Glycian we heard the lamentation of the Snow Chanter. Our far mother still abides within the Wild, but she is trapped and helpless, and she summons us to aid her."

Bennek saw that these words troubled Lanyon. He told her, "Lanyon, you must not fear the Snow Chanter. You asked before if we knew of any Inyomere who had forsworn the blasphemy of Siddél. Tayeraisa the Snow Chanter is one. She is the blessed mother of our clan and was always a friend of the people. That has not changed, and it will not change when we find her and release her from her plight."

"I confess I am frightened and full of wonder too. Do you know where she is? Do you know what has become of her?"

Marshal spoke first. "Our dreams beckon us to the high country of the Tiyat-kel. The Snow Chanter is entrapped there, and it is our task to free her."

Kit added, "We haven't seen the way with certainty. Our far mother is weak, but she still calls to us, and we will find her."

As they spoke, Bennek resumed his search, determined to unravel the mystery of the unwholesome presence. But as he circled behind Lanyon he realized to his consternation that he had circled behind the wicked presence too.

Marshal noticed his perplexed look. "Bennek? Is there something you sense?"

Lanyon turned. Her eyes flared in surprise to find him behind her.

Bennek met her frightened gaze. "There is something wicked here," he said. "Some dreadful power. At first I thought it was an Inyomere. But now I think it is something else."

Marshal stepped backward, reaching for his sword. Kit shifted sideways with an anxious glance around the hollow. Lanyon stood without moving, but panic stirred in her eyes.

Bennek sought to reassure her. "You must not fear us. We are honorable men."

"I do not question your honor."

"Help me to understand this evil. It is not you . . . yet it is of you."

She bit her lip. Struggling with indecision, she looked again at Marshal and Kit, but in the end she spoke to Bennek. "You sense the talisman I carry. It is a wicked thing."

"I don't understand. What is a talisman?"

"It's an object bound to a spell."

Bennek had never heard of such a thing, but then he knew almost nothing of spells and sorcery. "If it's wicked, why don't you throw it away?"

This suggestion horrified her. "Oh, no. It was made for a special purpose. *Not* by me. I wish it had never been made! But it was left to me and I *will* use it."

"But what is its purpose?"

She hesitated, but Kit was eager to know as well. He said, "You don't need to fear us, Lanyon Kyramanthes, and it may be we can help you after we've rescued the Snow Chanter. We are good fighters, but more than that, we survive in the Wild because Bennek has a bit of the magic of the Inyomere in him. In the hunt he has a knack of confusing the minds of the arowl, and this gives us great advantage."

A compliment? It stunned Bennek to hear such.

Kit took no notice, asking Lanyon, "Please, won't you tell us why you've come to Samokea?"

Marshal urged her too, "Yes, please speak."

She nodded, wide-eyed, as if astonished at her own willingness to trust them. "I will tell you. I'm only passing through this land as quickly as I may. I was asleep on this hill when your hunt commenced. I've taken to walking all night when the arowl are less wakeful. I'm on my way to the far north to slay the Inyomere Siddél."

Bennek looked on, awestruck. Then he turned to his brother. "Marshal! Why didn't we think to do this?"

Marshal shared his wonder. "I fear we are too timid."

Lanyon read them wrong. She thought they teased her. "You doubt me," she concluded sadly. "I don't blame you."

"Lanyon Kyramanthes, we do not," Marshal insisted. "It's just that... well, Siddél is the greatest—no, the most terrible Inyomere."

Kit spoke in warm anger. "Siddél created the blasphemy of the arowl! He gave them life, and released them in their madness on the Wild!"

Bennek echoed his outrage. "Siddél destroyed Samokea! He murdered our Chieftain Édan, and sent the arowl ravening across Samokea so that our people were forced to flee. He is our greatest enemy, and we will aid you in his destruction, Lanyon, after we have found the Snow Chanter."

All swiftly agreed to this, but Kit still wanted to know, "How is such a thing to be done? Siddél is no petty Inyomere. He is the storm. He's not bound to any place, but wanders all the Wild. Slaying him is like slaying a great thunderstorm. Is such a thing possible? Even for you, Lanyon? You have an Inyomere's magic, but Siddél—"

"It is possible." She touched one of the two straps that crisscrossed her chest—the one that held the bundle. "Here is the talisman I carry. It's an arrow, and it was made with the singular purpose of slaying Siddél—to pierce not just his heart, but his soul, and so separate him from this world. It is my task to find his home in the north, the Storm Lair where he dwells when he is not at work terrorizing the Wild. There I will lie in wait for him and kill him when he comes."

Marshal had a faraway look.

Kit sighed in sweet contentment.

Bennek grinned. "I think we have not met by chance."

"May we accompany you, then?" Kit asked.

Hope shone in her clear face, and she smiled with quiet joy. "Yes. Let us fare together, as fate allows."

# 4

They walked north through a country of low, rocky hills, and as before, they stopped now and then so that Bennek could seek for arowl. This skill fascinated Lanyon, while Bennek expressed astonishment that she—with the power to set the heart of an arowl on fire—could not do this simple thing.

Lanyon answered him, turning her hands palm-up. "It's in your nature so it seems easy to you, but I think it is a rare gift."

Though she had been afoot all night she showed no weariness, walking at a fast clip to keep up with the boys' longer strides. The hem of her night-black robe trailed in the grass, its dense weave sliding over sticks and brambles without catching. A flush of exertion highlighted her cheeks; her eyes were bright and warm—and Bennek was not unhappy to find himself the subject of her gaze as they walked along.

"I am admiring your pendant," she confessed with a smile. "There's a smith in the Citadel of the Snow Chanter—" She caught herself as she realized her mistake. A frown of confusion replaced her smile. "Forgive me, I'm rambling. There *was* a smith who worked in just this style. I only wondered if this might be her work . . . but I know she crossed over long ago."

Bennek touched the pendant—a blazing sun rising into a shallow triangle of twining vines. "My far mother wore this as she fled the Citadel."

"Ah, it *is* old then . . . and you have brought it back to Samokea. Bennek, your far mother would be proud."

He grinned. He could not help himself.

The gray clouds that had begun the day grew heavier as the hours passed until their soft bellies brushed the hilltops, casting the early afternoon into gloom. Yet the mood of the boys remained bright, for in Lanyon Kyramanthes they had found something strange and marvelous.

Still, Marshal felt obliged to remind them of their peril. "Don't forget we have an unfinished battle. Just because we hope to put off our hunt until the evening, that doesn't mean the arowl won't try to find us sooner. Don't allow yourselves to be distracted."

Kit glanced at Lanyon and laughed. "Your warning comes too late, I think."

Lanyon sounded puzzled when she asked, "Do you still intend to hunt those arowl?"

"Indeed," Marshal answered. "We won't leave off until the task is done."

"But the survivors fled south, while we're going north. You'll never catch them this way."

"They will come after us," Marshal assured her. "They ran because they were panicked, but even now the lure of our flesh is working on them. Sometime today they will circle around, hoping to take us by surprise, but once again we'll have a surprise for them."

Lanyon cast an uneasy glance behind. "And why should you wait until evening? Surely it's harder to hunt them in the dark?"

"No, it's easier," Bennek insisted. "As you have said, the night is their time to sleep and they become sluggish, so it's less work to run them down—though they see better than we do. There is a danger from their bows."

"They can't shoot if they're running," Kit amended. "So we make sure to keep pushing them."

Bennek flashed a bloodthirsty grin. "Eventually one will stumble." He reached to his shoulder and seized the hilt of his sword, sweeping it out of its scabbard and making as if to hack at the ground. "They don't get up again."

Bennek puzzled over the mystery of Lanyon, and the more he thought on it, the more peculiarities he found.

There was her sorcery. Bennek was Samokeän and had his own gifts, yet he had never heard of anyone who could slay the arowl with only a thought, except for the Chieftain Édan.

There was the evil talisman she carried, its wicked presence a shadow lurking at the edge of his mind.

And her lineage . . .

Kyramanthes was the most ancient clan to descend from the children of Jahallon-the-Undying, but in Habaddon that bloodline was said to have died out over a hundred years ago, in the days when Édan was still chieftain in Samokea.

Next there were her garments, which looked as if they had been made for the death rites of a beloved chieftain, and not for an expedition in Samokea. Her shoes were slight, without hard soles, like the house slippers worn by some of the wise women of Habaddon.

And then there was the strange lilt of her speech.

And her size—she seemed slight and fragile when measured against the women of Samokea and Habaddon.

Finally—but certainly not least of all these things—how to explain her bold venture through the arowl-ravaged lands of Samokea, where her path had, by chance, joined that of the only three men to venture so far beyond the Glycian River in years upon troubled years.

In midafternoon they climbed to the top of a ridge where they could rest with a good view of the surrounding land. Lanyon shared out dried venison from her field kit, while Marshal told her of their family and of the summer his father and Kit's had not come home.

"They had gone crusading with Jahallon in the spring. Bennek was born in the early summer. He was only two days in the world when my mother's brother came to tell us that both men had fallen in battle."

Lanyon looked to Bennek, who sat on the side, honing one of his knives. "So he never saw you."

"We were never in the world together," Bennek said, without pausing in his work. "He was already dead when I was born."

She nodded her sympathy. "And your mothers? What became of them?"

Marshal said, "They stayed on at our family keep. My uncle begged them to come away and live with him in his own keep closer to Habaddon, but they refused."

"They were strong," Kit said. "They knew how to defend our keep. They taught us to fight."

Marshal nodded his agreement. "And they taught us the history of Samokea, and how to read and write . . . but finally they fell to the arowl."

"They were consumed by the arowl," Bennek amended, each stroke of his knife precise against the whetstone.

"Bennek saw it," Marshal acknowledged. "He was eight, and they had taken him hunting. They were following a family of forest buffalo . . . but an arowl pack had lately come into Fathalia, and it was stalking the same prey."

Lanyon turned a troubled gaze on Bennek. "How did you escape?"

His hands held to their steady rhythm as he answered in a matter-of-fact voice. "They told me to run to the Glycian River and throw myself in. So I did it. The river was a torrent. It took me a day and a night to walk home."

He felt the weight of Marshal's gaze but did not respond to it, and after a few seconds, Marshal shook his head, saying, "Bennek will never admit to being sad."

"I never am sad," Bennek answered sharply. "What is there to be sad about? My mother and father are together, and someday I'll be with them. In the meantime, I kill arowl."

"Is that when you learned to confound the arowl?" Lanyon asked him. "When you were fleeing to the river?"

Bennek stopped his grinding. He looked up at her in surprise. "Is this true?" Marshal asked him curiously. "You have never said."

"It's not something I think on." He returned to his work.

Lanyon told them, "My story is not so different from yours, though I was eleven when my father died. We lived in Ohtangia then, in a fort in the high mountains. He too had gone with Jahallon to campaign against the arowl, and all my brothers went with him. None of them came back."

"I am sorry for your family," Bennek said. "Do any of Clan Kyramanthes still live in Ohtangia?"

"No, I am the last. So you were nearly right that Kyramanthes is extinguished."

"How is it the talents of the Inyomere are so strong in you?" Kit wondered. "Could you be Samokeän, at least in part?"

She shrugged. "The descendants of Samoket and Kyramanthes have mingled many times."

Once again Bennek stopped in his work, but now he looked at her in delight. "Then you are our far cousin! You have Samokeän blood, and are a descendant of the Snow Chanter too."

She smiled politely and made a little bow. "I offer greetings to my far cousins."

Bennek considered this further. "So you have the blood of the Snow Chanter, but you are also Kyramanthes, and that is the oldest clan, descendant of Jahallon's first child . . . and the curse of the Inyomere Siddél is on Jahallon-the-Undying and from him it passed in greatest force to Kyramanthes, and through that bloodline some great talent has come to you . . . and will descend through you." His mood shifted to one of speculation. "You are not married yet?"

"Bennek!" Marshal protested.

But Lanyon pressed a hand against her mouth and laughed. "That is blood *lust*."

"So you are not married?"

"You ask very many questions."

"Then you are married," Bennek concluded with disappointment.

"I have been married. I am married no longer."

"What does that mean?"

"It means we offer our condolences," Marshal said.

"Oh." Bennek set the knife aside and bowed his head to her. "Truly, I am sorry for your loss ... but I am wondering too—is this fire spell something you can teach?"

"It was taught to me."

"I would learn it."

She nodded. "When there is time, I'll teach you its name."

They came upon the River Talahnon in late afternoon. Its course had turned northwest so they followed it, walking on a low bluff above a floodplain filled with rustling cane grass.

They saw many birds and a few rabbits, and once they saw a small wildcat, but they found no signs of larger creatures. The horses and deer, the antelope, the hardy cattle and the buffalo that had once grazed the green fields of Samokea were gone. The arowl had run unopposed in that land since the fall of Édan, hunting to extinction the vast herds that once lived there.

The bluff came to an end, and they found themselves walking along the edge of the cane, with the great stalks swaying and rustling above their heads.

As the afternoon waned, the air grew heavy and cold, and a mist was born. It came out of the cane and up from the ground in drifts and tendrils that blended together, enveloping them. Fine droplets of water gathered on their hair and eyelashes. They could not see far so they took care to step softly, listening for any sound more mysterious than the call of birds or the rustle of rats.

Bennek had still not discovered any arowl and this seemed strange to him. He asked to stop. And while Marshal and Kit stood watch, he sent his spirit-self wandering farther than he had before. He searched among the hills and along the riverbanks. But he couldn't find arowl anywhere within his reach and the effort left him dizzy, as if he had leaned too far over a fortress wall and nearly tumbled off.

He still felt muzzy-headed as they set out again. It didn't help that the mist blurred the landscape and lent his ears a ghostly imagination, so that he heard all around him a sourceless whispering, a faint, frantic warning, repeating, repeating, over and over again.

Lanyon stopped. She gazed at the cane, her eyes wide with fright. "Do any of you hear her? Can you hear the mist speaking?"

"Is she real?" Bennek asked in surprise.

Kit, who stood behind him, said, "I can hear her. She is a morbid Inyomere, though I don't think she means us harm."

Marshal nodded. "Let her do no worse than this and we won't complain."

Lanyon shook her head. "We must not disregard her. I will not do so again."

"But what does she say?" Kit wanted to know. "I can't understand her."

"Nor can I," Marshal said. "Her words run together. It's maddening to hear her murmurous voice and yet hear no meaning."

Bennek frowned. He heard it differently. In a puzzled voice he told them, "*He is coming.* That's what she says. She repeats it over and over. *He is coming. He is coming. He is coming.*"

Lanyon stared at him with wide eyes.

Then from deep in the cane there came a sudden loud rustle.

Marshal heard it and swept his sword from its scabbard. "*Bennek?*"

"It is not arowl."

Kit hauled out his bow and nocked an arrow. "A tiger, then? They will most often dwell beside the water."

Bennek slipped his spear from its scabbard and twisted on the extension. "I will look." He advanced on the cane. Marshal stepped up beside him—and at once they heard the sound of a large beast crashing away toward the river.

Bennek started after it, wanting to know what it was, but Lanyon appeared beside him. She caught his arm, speaking words that confused him. "Please stop! Bennek, don't kill him."

"*What?*"

She pushed past, plunging ahead along a path of broken cane that marked the creature's retreat.

What madness had come over her? Was it her purpose to come up against a tiger unarmed? Bennek darted after her. He didn't dare call out—it was not their way to imitate the hue and cry of the arowl—but as he ran to catch her, he begged her silently to *stop, stop, stop!*

And it seemed she heard him. She turned around with a look of astonishment, and he caught her. He seized her arm as she had seized his. "Do not go on!" he commanded in a fierce whisper.

She didn't speak. She made no sound. Yet very clearly he heard her voice inside his head asking, *Who are you?*

Marshal slipped past them and Lanyon turned, reaching out as if to stop him. But just then they heard a splash. Marshal froze. He stared ahead, but nothing could be seen except the cane and the mist.

"It has gone into the river," he concluded, turning a mistrustful gaze on Lanyon. "Did you see what it was?"

She stared ahead, at nothing. "I thought I saw someone. It was what the Inyomere said. 'He is coming.' It made me think someone was there."

Kit came up behind them. In his fingers he held a few strands of downy gray hair. "I think it was a wolf."

Lanyon looked as if she had a different opinion, but all she said was, "I am sorry to have caused you trouble."

"The Inyomere has made us all nervous," Marshal told her gently.

"I wish she would relent," Kit said. Then, with an irreverent grin, he called out to the mist, "Blessed One, we understand he is still coming, whoever *he* might be."

They went on. Bennek walked with Lanyon. He wanted to ask what it meant that he had heard her unspoken voice; he wanted her to say she had heard his, but he didn't want Marshal or Kit to know it, so he kept his silence.

The day grew old, but the mist did not recede and neither did the Inyomere's tedious, whispered warning. It wore on their nerves so that when a distant baying arose from across the river, they all startled. Kit and Marshal both reached for their weapons.

But Bennek insisted it was not arowl. "Perhaps it's a wild dog, though I don't know."

"And where *are* the arowl?" Kit wondered. "They've tarried so long I expect there's some mischief in it."

Evening was not far off when the cane gave way to a rocky shoreline. A little farther on, they sighted a steep bluff looming out of the mist. Low thickets and scattered groves of small hardy trees clothed its face. A narrow beach divided it from the water.

Marshal said, "We can make a defense here, if we need to. At the least we should be able to find some sheltered place to spend the night."

They climbed the bluff. The mist thinned as they got higher, and soon they were above it. From the top they looked out on the mist-shrouded line of the river and the dark plains beyond. Bats fluttered in the twilight and crickets sang an evening chorus. The river murmured in its bed. And far off, faint, there only when they held their breath, came the howl and yammering of a distant pack.

"Ah, there they are," Kit said softly. "They're warming up. Working up their rage. They will be silent soon, when they begin the hunt."

Bennek closed his eyes and slipped into the spirit-world, but he could not find them, they were that far, and again he was left with the dizzying feeling that he had pitched himself over a precipice. Still, he did not doubt they would come. The arowl were a corruption made to prey upon the people, forever driven by a fierce desire for the blood of men and women. They could not resist it.

# 5

Darkness gathered as they prepared a camp. They had found a hollow, sheltered beneath an overhang and surrounded by a hedge of low brush. Bennek gathered wood for a fire, but he didn't light it. Lanyon went down alone to the stream. She was gone some time. But just as Bennek began to worry for her, she returned, carrying a net of knotted sedges holding a fine catch of fish. She hung the net from a gnarled tree while the boys counted up their arrows. Then they all settled down to wait.

The mist had left every leaf and twig and blade of grass heavy with dew. The fitful patter of falling droplets filled the night. An hour passed. They chewed on the last of the dried venison Lanyon had carried. Then Kit stretched out on the strip of dry ground beneath the overhang and slept. Most of another hour went by. The mist dissipated, and the stars shone out brightly. Lanyon began a soft chant.

At once, Kit awoke, and like Marshal and Bennek, he listened.

The words were indistinct: faint nonsense syllables slurred together in a rhythm that repeated over and over. Soon the boys sensed a warm presence closing around them. "What spell is this?" Marshal whispered.

Lanyon didn't answer; her chant did not falter as minute after minute crept past.

Then Bennek spoke out of the shadows. "The arowl have found

our trail. They're still some miles south, but they move swiftly, and in stealth." His gear rustled as he stood up and stepped into the open. "They have found companions. There are nine now. All are on this side of the river, but they do not repeat their mistake of this morning. They are spread out, and I won't be able to confound them all."

"Then we'll stay together," Marshal said.

Kit drew a sharp breath. "What strangeness has descended on us?" He too slipped out from beneath the sheltering stone. "The stars are bright and I have always seen well in the night, yet my eyes play tricks on me. I can see the thickets and the rocks, but you Bennek, I scarcely can see, though . . . I think . . . is this your shape here in the fullness of the starlight?" He reached out to assure himself he had indeed found his cousin, and Bennek startled at his unexpected touch.

"Kit, you are but a glimmer!"

Marshal half-rose. "Both of you can scarcely be seen. Lanyon, speak to us. Is this your spell?"

They turned to her, and alone among them she seemed substantial: a shadow of deepest black within the gray shadows that filled the hollow. She still chanted, though her voice had gone hoarse. Bennek had long-since memorized her repeated verse, and he mouthed the last syllables as she neared the end. She did not begin again.

"Lanyon?" Marshal asked.

A soft sigh escaped her. "I have put an enchantment on all of you." She sounded very tired. "It's a spell of concealment called the Hunter's Veil. Despite their keen vision in the dark, it will be difficult for the arowl to see you, just as it's hard for you to see them at night. And the sounds you make will be muffled in their ears."

Kit laughed. "This should be short work."

"If they don't flee," Marshal cautioned. "We must slay them all tonight, or they will find even more of their kind to come after us."

"It's not all good," Lanyon said as she joined them in the starlight. "I don't know how to affect their animal senses, so they will still be able to track you by scent."

"We'll be cautious," Marshal assured her.

She walked with them a little way, until she could look out on the river, where not a tendril of mist remained. Starlight glittered on the water and in the dew that clung to the trees and thickets, but despite this generous illumination the three young warriors could hardly be seen unless they moved, and even then the eye slipped away from the uncertainty of their shapes.

"It's a bright night," Kit whispered. "Lanyon, did you also send the clouds away?"

"Kit, you must not speak thus!" she said, sounding scandalized. "This is a gift of the Inyomere of the mist."

"She that howled at us all this afternoon?"

"She is sad, I think, remembering what is past. But this night she gives her blessing."

This drew from Kit a soft chuckle. "Ah, where would we be without the kindness of the Inyomere? For though they despise us, they hate the arowl even more."

"Let's go," Bennek said impatiently, and, taking his own advice, he set off first into the glittering night.

Marshal beckoned them together beside the river, where they appeared as a trio of ghostly shapes. In a whisper he warned them again, "Do not be distracted by this woman or made over-confident by her gifts. There is great mystery about her, but I don't think she has contested much with the arowl before this day. In any case, her sorcery has drained her. If you are in a tight spot, you must save yourself."

"Well then," Kit whispered, "Bennek is doomed."

"Doomed to rescue you, no doubt."

"Oh good," Marshal said. "We are as always, then."

At first he led them southeast along the river, but after a quarter mile he turned away from the water and entered a place of scattered boulders, many twice his own height, that must have rolled off the bluff in the beginning of the world. Between the boulders grew many short trees with knobby trunks and slender branches that held crowns of tiny leaves up to the stars. Amid the lacy shadows the three of them all but disappeared. Marshal had to sign three times before Kit and Bennek perceived his gesture to halt.

After that he resorted to whispering. Pulling Bennek close, he spoke into his ear—"Find them"—in words hardly louder than a breath.

Bennek nodded. Crouching with his back to a boulder, he closed his eyes and sent his sight questing outward—but a moment later he stood up again. The arowl had come much sooner than he'd expected. Pointing back to the river, he held up four fingers, waving his hand to be sure that Marshal could see.

Marshal whispered, "The other five?"

Bennek waved vaguely to the south, *Not close enough to worry us yet.*

Marshal wanted a better defensive position. Nudging Bennek and Kit to follow, he set out again, and soon came to a largish mound covered in tumbled boulders gleaming white in the starlight. To the south was a patch of open ground, while to the east and west more trees of humble stature marched up to the mound's foot. They climbed the slope and hid themselves among the rocks. Kit set an arrow to his bowstring.

Marshal turned to Bennek and gave his whispered instruction. "Wait for the arowl. When they draw near, confound them."

Bennek did not want to do it. He was always confounded himself for several seconds after working his will on the arowl, and such a delay would let Kit and Marshal dominate the count. If the pack was large, he would make no complaint, but there were not so many tonight. "Marshal, we don't need to confound them. They are only four—and all on four feet—there are no were-beasts among them!"

Marshal wasn't swayed. "Do as I ask and do not argue."

So, with a disgruntled expression safely hidden by the darkness and the Hunter's Veil, Bennek settled himself against the ground, closed his eyes, and with his spirit sight went seeking the four arowl.

They had separated. Three hung back, waiting on a call to hunt.

The fourth pursued their scent trail. It had a long, low, sinuous body, reminiscent of a weasel but many times larger. Bennek was a ghost, gliding invisibly beside it as it passed nimbly through the brush. Only when it came within easy range of Kit's arrow did he affect it. Then he filled up its mind with dread, and it sat back and howled.

The quiet of the night was undone. An answering clamor came from the three hidden arowl as Kit released an arrow, silencing the dazed tracker.

Bennek let his awareness slide until he met the leader of the oncoming three. It was another like the tracker. This one, though, raced toward the rocks as if it already knew where they were hidden.

Bennek confounded it just as it came into sight. Kit quickly shot it, but needed a second arrow to bring it down.

The next arowl reached the foot of the mound before Bennek countered it. The stunned beast turned to retreat. Marshal went after it with his sword. He ran it down and slew it, then turned and impaled the fourth beast as it leaped at him from the shelter of the trees.

So Kit and Marshal were two and two while Bennek's kills numbered zero. He tried not to dwell on the injustice of it, for now the dreadful howls of more hunting arowl sounded from the south. Some rang loudly in the night, but more could be heard in the far distance. Bennek sent his awareness out among them.

These arowl had learned from the morning's battle. They did not hunt in a tight pack, staying far apart instead, so Bennek could not affect them all at once. He tried to count their number, but they moved swiftly. Before he could find them all, an arrow cracked against the rocks.

Kit shook him hard. "Wake up! The main pack is here. It's a real battle now."

More arrows hissed from out of the trees to the south.

"This is not the main pack," Bennek warned. "These are the five I counted before, but a second pack comes perhaps a mile behind them."

"And how many are they?"

"Six more at least, but I couldn't finish a count."

Marshal had returned to shelter in the boulders at the foot of the mound. Kit called the news down to him.

"Fan out then," Marshal told them. "We'll finish the five, before we start the next round."

This order was to Bennek's liking. He obeyed at once, creeping silently away into the shadows of the trees, darting from one patch of deep darkness to the next in a staggered run toward the shelter of another tumble of boulders. He had almost made it when a foul scent reached him, carried by a friendly breeze.

He ducked down into dense shadow as two arowl appeared from around the rocks, one a small were-beast of uncertain lineage and the other a great wolf of unnatural size.

Bennek stared at the wolf in astonishment. Never had he seen such a creature before. Its four legs were as long as his own and he could not have gotten his arms around its massive head—not that he wanted to. The wolf's long shaggy coat reeked beyond the foulest arowl Bennek had ever encountered. A dire wolf, that certainly had not been with the pack they'd hunted that morning.

The great beast did not seem to see Bennek. But as it huffed once, twice, its hot breath steaming in the night, he knew that in a moment it would find his scent. He had only this moment to use the element of surprise. So, hefting his spear, he charged.

The wolf saw him then. It bared its great teeth and bounded to meet him. The small were-beast had scrambled to ready an arrow, but it could not shoot with the wolf in its line of fire.

Bennek dropped into a crouch. The great beast leaped at him. He cast his spear into its chest. Then he rolled aside as the dire wolf crashed past him, scrambling behind the shelter of a tree to shield himself from the arrows of the were-beast.

The wolf fell to the ground but it did not stay down. With a great heave of its shoulders, it surged to its feet and turned to find him. The long shaft of Bennek's spear protruded from its chest.

That spear was Bennek's favorite weapon and he wanted it back unbroken. So he charged the wolf again, this time seizing the shaft with both hands. The beast flinched back, looking startled, as if Bennek had appeared out of nowhere. He used the moment to yank the spear out of its chest. Blood flooded from the wound and the wolf staggered backward, its great jaws snapping blindly at air.

Shifting his grip, Bennek stepped in close and thrust up, driving the spear through the back of the wolf's jaw and into its brain. Blood gushed on him as he yanked it out again. He had to jump aside to avoid being crushed as the great wolf collapsed to the ground.

Marshal wanted to follow Bennek into the trees, but in his forward position on the mound, every movement he made drew a well-placed arrow. He answered the assault with arrows of his own, but it was a guessing game. The arowl archers had not yet shown themselves. After a minute Kit called down to him, "We have no time for this. Make ready, and I'll flush them out for you."

Kit slipped away from the ridge, circling around to the west. Silently, he entered the grove where the arowl archers were hidden. He heard the *thwak* of their bows and then, from behind him, a rustle of fallen leaves. He spun around.

Just steps away, glimmering gray in the starlight, stood a huge dog, as tall as his elbow. It had a broad head and a long, powerful muzzle. Its tail wagged slowly as it watched him.

Not for a moment did Kit mistake such a handsome creature for an arowl. He knew it for a true dog, of the kind that ran with Jahallon's armies.

He started to speak to it, but just then a horrific growling-howl erupted from the west, beyond the ridge. The dog ducked out of sight, and Kit remembered that Bennek had gone that way alone.

"Ben-nek!" he bellowed, "you bet-ter be a-wake!"

He plunged amid the trees, still screaming and bellowing in his most fearsome voice.

The tactic worked. A small arowl with a bow started up from the shadows. Kit charged it, but it was faster, skipping out of the trees and into the open, where Marshal dropped it with a single arrow.

---

When the wolf fell, Bennek turned to look for the second arowl. He didn't have to look far. The were-beast had come up behind him. It had an arrow nocked, and by its manner it was clear the beast knew he was somewhere about, yet it did not see him. It blinked frantically and its aim shifted, now closer, now farther, defeated by the Hunter's Veil.

Bennek did not hesitate. He hurled his spear at its chest, then dropped to the ground. An arrow whizzed past overhead as the arowl cried out once, and fell.

Marshal was certain there had been at least two archers among the trees. He waited five seconds, then ten, for another arowl to flee from Kit's assault, but when Kit appeared at the edge of the grove, he knew the plan had failed.

Lanyon's spell still made Kit's shape an uncertain glimmer, but the enchantment of the Hunter's Veil had begun to fade, and Marshal marked him easily—as did the arowl that lay in wait among the branches above Kit's head.

A flash of motion among the leaves was their only warning.

"Above you!" Marshal shouted, but the arowl had already dropped.

Still, his shout gave Kit a moment to prepare. He met the arowl with his sword, slicing it across its belly. Its onrushing weight knocked him to the ground. He rolled away from it, and then he turned, and with his sword he hammered at its head.

Marshal bounded up to him. "Are you hurt?"

"Drowned in arowl blood. How's the baby?"

Just then Bennek bellowed, "My count is two!" With a glimmer of motion, he stepped into sight on the other side of the patch of open ground. "One is a very great arowl that I didn't see this morning."

Kit called back to him, "Have a care! We felled only two ourselves, leaving one—"

He broke off as a frightful snarling erupted from deep within the trees. There followed a panicked screech, and then silence, save for the fearful howling of the second pack. Marshal and Kit traded a startled look.

Then Kit remembered, "I saw a dog of the kind that goes to war with the men of Habaddon. I think it must have been the 'wolf' we heard within the cane."

"I just hope it doesn't hunt us too," Marshal said. Then to Bennek, "We need to know what's out there."

"The pack is nigh!" Bennek objected. "There isn't time."

"We will cover you! Bennek, we need to know."

So Bennek retreated again into the trees, where he crouched in the deepest shadows, trying to quiet his heart.

The howling of the approaching pack was blood-chilling.

"Listen to it," Kit said, as he and Marshal retrieved arrows from the arowl corpses. "Bennek is right. There are likely more than six—but this time they howl in one chorus."

Marshal nodded. "Instinct has beaten strategy, and once again they're running as a pack. Come. Let's return to the position in the rocks. *Now*, I think." For the pack was almost upon them.

"Bennek!" Marshal shouted. "Come join us."

Bennek didn't answer.

"He's entranced," Kit said.

"Ben-nek!"

"I'll get him."

"No. Get into the rocks. Bring down as many as you can with your bow. I'll wake him."

So Kit returned to the mound, while Marshal took off for the trees where Bennek had disappeared. "Bennek! Bennek, wake up. Answer me."

Through the trees, Marshal glimpsed the oncoming pack. Seven arowl, at least, and four of them were-beasts on two feet. Kit would soon be overwhelmed.

But then the tone of the howls changed and the arowl ceased their advance. They hesitated among the trees, turning about, appearing confused, uncertain, in that way Marshal had seen many times before. "Good, Bennek," he said softly.

Kit shot first, then Marshal a moment later. Four arowl fell in the first few seconds and the remaining three—all of them were-beasts—fled howling toward the river.

Bennek turned up, looking furious. "You've chased them off, haven't you?"

"We brought down four!" Kit said in their defense.

"Only because I stunned them for you!"

Marshal was already at work, pulling arrows from the corpses. "Are there more, Bennek?"

"No. Just those three—and at least one of them is going to be mine!" He hefted his spear and set off after them, with Marshal and Kit close behind.

The night remained brilliant, the air quite still. The remaining arowl were easy to follow because in their panic, they cried out instinctively for aid.

Bennek ran hard, determined to catch up to them before they crossed the river, but they surprised him with a sudden turn north . . . as if they had caught a new scent. At the same time, the tone of their howls changed, becoming bold and bloodthirsty again.

"They are on the hunt ," Kit warned.

Marshal answered him, "They've discovered Lanyon!"

"We must protect her," Bennek panted. "She's weary. She may not be able to defend herself."

They turned north toward the bluff, racing through the trees, weaving past the boulders, determined to cut off the three arowl. As they ran, the enchantment that had hidden them wore away.

By the time they plunged out of the trees and into the crackling brush at the foot of the bluff, the three arowl, which had just come bounding up from the river, were able to see them clearly: Bennek with his spear, and Kit and Marshal with swords drawn.

The were-beasts each carried swords of their own. The intoxicating scent of their prey, so very near, drove away all vestige of their earlier terror. They lunged for the boys. Screams and howls filled the night, punctuated by the jarring clang of sword on sword.

Kit finished his beast in three strokes. Marshal's lasted only two before it turned and fled back toward the water so that he had to run it down. But Bennek's had some skill.

It was a black were-wolf, its face screwed up in a ferocious snarl as it parried Bennek's spear thrusts. Starlight sparkled on its long white teeth.

Kit came up, dancing in and out with his sword, striking at its side to harry it. In desperation, it threw itself at Bennek.

That was the move he'd waited for. He dropped to one knee, bracing the end of his spear against the ground, ready to catch the wolf on the blade.

But in that moment Lanyon screamed in horror— "*No!*" —and the heart of the wolf caught fire. Bennek speared it anyway, heaving it up and over his head before hurling it to the ground. The flame glowed—it did not blaze like the fire that had taken the two arowl in the morning—but it had erupted deep in the heart, killing the beast at once, so that it was a dead thing he skewered.

He yanked his spear out of the corpse and glared upslope, where Lanyon stood, wide-eyed and breathing hard. "I do not need help in the killing of arowl!" he told her.

Her mouth opened and closed before she spoke in a small voice. "I am sorry. It frightened me."

"You must think better of me."

"I will. I do."

Bennek was hardly mollified. He stomped off to see how Marshal had dispatched his mark, leaving Kit smirking behind him.

# 6

It was well past midnight when they dragged the corpses of the three dead arowl to the water and dumped them in the river. Afterward, they stripped off their gear and cleaned it of blood. Then they washed themselves in the icy water. Bennek had to unbraid his hair and scrub his scalp with sand to get out the dried blood of the giant wolf, so he was last to return to the bluff.

As he climbed to the hollow, he caught the scent of woodsmoke and roasting fish. Feeling suddenly famished, he picked up his pace. He found Lanyon, Marshal, and Kit all sitting around a low fire, where neatly filleted fish roasted on steaming green sticks.

"Ah, I forgot about food," he whispered, feeling as if he might swoon.

"Fortunately, Lanyon did not," Kit said. "You'll have to forgive her for killing your arowl."

"I'm sorry I was angry."

She lifted a stick from the fire and handed it to him with a somber expression. "I'm sorry I was not brave."

As they described the hunt to her, Kit remembered the dog he had seen. "I think it's curious about us. Certainly it showed no hostility toward me, though its feelings for the arowl were less kind."

Marshal laughed. "That is true! Never have I been rewarded with such a fear-filled screech from any arowl *I* have cornered."

"It's strange to find it here," Kit mused as he shoved a green stick—now empty of fish—into the coals, and helped himself to another. "I wonder if its kind has lived wild in Samokea since the fall of Édan?"

Lanyon turned away from the firelight. In a mournful tone she said, "I think it must have lost its master. If so, it may finally come to us."

Bennek sensed some personal grief behind her words. "Lanyon, have you seen this dog before?"

She shrugged. "Jahallon's scouts will often take such a dog with them, for they are trained to hunt the arowl and to give warning at their approach."

"Much like Bennek," Kit said, earning a guffaw from Marshal, but also a stinging bit of gravel against the side of his head.

The last of the fish soon disappeared. Lanyon built up the fire, while Bennek described the great wolf he had battled. "I never saw anything like it before."

"It is Siddél's art to conjure monsters," Lanyon said bitterly.

"He is skilled at it," Kit agreed. "The beasts he sends to devour us grow fiercer each year—and still we are not defeated."

"May it always be so." Lanyon arose and brought more wood to the fire. "I'll keep watch tonight, for all of you must be weary from the hunt."

Bennek and Kit did not need further persuasion. They found their blankets and were quickly asleep. Marshal, though, sat watching the fire. Lanyon waited, but when he did not speak, she crouched by his side. "You are wondering if you can trust me."

"We only met today, and you are full of mystery."

"I haven't spoken all the secrets of my life, but please believe that we are friends, and that I would never bring harm to you, or any of the people."

"There is something I must know. It's been on my mind all day."

She drew back a little, but nodded.

"Did you have a baby?"

She flinched. Several seconds passed, and he thought she would not answer, but finally she said, "I had two. My son was one and a half years in the world. My daughter was new-born. They were slain, and my husband too, when Siddél attacked our household. How did you know?"

"There's a faint scent of milk on your clothes."

"Still? And yet in my memory it was long ago." She sighed. "Marshal, do not feel sorry for me. Like Bennek, I am not sad. My babies have crossed over, and they are safe now from the evil of Siddél, and in good time I will be with them."

He nodded. "That is the comfort we all must keep."

"Will you let me watch?"

"Only if you promise to wake me in two hours."

"I promise. Now rest, so you will be ready should the arowl come again."

The arowl did not come.

Lanyon woke Marshal as promised then went to sleep herself, waking again at dawn. Finding Bennek on watch, she took him with her to check a line of rabbit traps. "We won't go far," she promised. "You'll know if anything ventures near camp."

"When did you have time to put out traps?"

"Last night, after you set off on the hunt."

The traps were neat cords made of braided sedges. She had placed twelve, but the first one, and then the second, turned up empty.

"Lanyon?" Bennek asked.

"Yes?"

"Yesterday by the river . . ."

"Oh."

"You asked me, 'Who are you?' I heard your voice, though you didn't speak."

"You surprised me, that's all. I know who you are. You are Bennek of Samokea, far son of the Snow Chanter, and many talents have come down to you."

The third trap too was empty, but Bennek hardly noticed. "Bennek of Samokea," he mused. "That was never my name . . . before."

Lanyon looked at him in confusion. "How then are you called?"

"Bennek of Clan Samoket."

"Oh. I am sorry. I mis-remembered it."

He shrugged. "All my people are named thus, since we live in Samokea no more. But you are from Ohtangia. It must be that our custom is not known there."

"It must be."

They went on, only to discover that the fourth rabbit trap also was empty, and the fifth and the sixth. Lanyon's disappointment was keen. Bennek tried to hide his own, for he felt half-starved and was sure there was very little left in their packs to eat.

"Bennek?"

"Yes?"

"You live in Samokea now."

He stopped and looked at her, not understanding.

She had a playful smile. "So I am right, and your true name *is* Bennek of Samokea." And she set off again, seeking the seventh trap which was empty, and also the eighth.

But Bennek was pleased. "Lanyon, you *are* right, and from now on I will be known as Bennek of Samokea."

She smiled at him. Then turning around again she said in surprise, "Oh look! We have caught a rabbit after all!"

Their luck had changed, and three of the last four traps had rabbits. Lanyon dispatched each quickly with a twist of the neck. Marshal carried a cooking pot, so she decided to cut them up and boil them. That was faster than roasting. When they returned to camp she sent Bennek to fetch water, and by the time the water was hot she had the rabbits neatly cubed, and was at work on the skins, scraping them clean.

Marshal still slept, but Kit had wakened. He took Bennek with him down to the battleground where they hunted for lost arrows. They stayed there three-quarters of an hour until finally Kit said, "Enough. We have found all but one, and if we don't return soon, Marshal shall have all the rabbit for himself."

"Come," Bennek said. "I would show you the wolf before we go."

They had to brave a choking stench to view the beast. It lay on its belly, head lolled on one side, just as it had fallen. Flies crawled in its eyes and across its blackened tongue. Daylight showed its pelt to be a dark, dirty gray, highlighted at each shoulder by a diagonal slash of the thin, white fur that grows back over scars. It was so large that even lying down, its great shoulders were level with Kit's chest.

He stared at it in amazement. He walked around it twice before he found his voice. "Oh my cousin, I confess I thought you exaggerated last night, but I was wrong." He bowed deeply from the waist, and the tribute was not lessened by the grin on his face. "You have bested us, at least in this round."

Bennek flushed with pleasure.

"But what's this?" Covering his nose against the stench, Kit stepped closer. Gingerly, he brushed back the dense fur around the wolf's neck. "It's a collar!"

Bennek went to look and it was just as Kit had said: the beast's neck was encircled by a tight-fitting iron collar, with a forged loop where a chain could be attached. Kit tugged at it to test its strength. Then he crooked a finger at Bennek. "Come."

They hurried away to fresher air.

"There's a mystery here," Kit said with a dark scowl. "This is not a were-beast, so why does it wear a collar? Who would dare to put one on such a dire wolf?"

Bennek shrugged. "Perhaps Siddél compelled the were-beasts to do it. Maybe these wolves must be chained to stop them destroying one another."

Kit looked doubtful, but for once he didn't argue.

Lanyon stretched the rabbit skins on small frames of greenwood that she carried with her when they set out again. She planned to work the skins into snug shoes that would serve her better than the house slippers she now wore.

All were tired, so they went slowly, following the River Talahnon. At first the river passed through a rocky land, but the crags soon fell behind them and they found themselves in the midst of a rolling prairie of waist-high grass. Now and then Bennek sought the arowl, but on that day, he found none.

As the afternoon wound down, Kit kept his bow ready and bagged three hen pheasants. They made camp while it was still light, in a grove of trees beside the river. Strawberries grew along the bank, and Lanyon spent the last of the daylight gathering all she could find. They ate well, and in the morning felt rested and ready for the day.

They continued north along the river, until a tributary flowing from the west cut across their path. Impatient to see the mountains, they decided to follow it. But by afternoon the tributary had lost its way, giving itself up to aimless wandering, so they crossed it and struck out to the northwest.

The land was beautiful yet desolate. Wind hissed through the tall grass, rolling it into shimmering waves that darkened, then brightened again as cloud shadows swept past. Pheasants called to one another, and chittering flocks of tiny finches whirled up from the grass at their approach. But of rabbits, foxes, and other such small creatures of the ground they saw no sign. Neither were there any trees, not even along the banks of the tiny creeks they discovered snaking through the grass. Kit didn't bother to hunt, since there was no wood to make a fire.

They made camp at twilight by treading out a circle in the tall grass near the bank of a stream. The wind had gone with the sun, leaving behind a silence tempered only by the murmuring voice of the stream as it spoke to itself in a glassy whisper.

"This is a gloomy place," Bennek said. "It feels hollow and ill-tempered, like an abandoned keep."

"I feel it too," Marshal said. "I've been plagued by a sense of foreboding ever since the light began to fade. We are not wanted here."

They ate in silence, a dreary meal of dried nuts that Marshal had carried all the way from Habaddon. A chill breeze sighed through the grass, setting the seed heads nodding in graceful silhouette against the starry sky.

"Am I alone?" Kit asked suddenly. "Can none of you feel the

anger here? Can you not hear it in the clatter of the water? In the hiss of the wind?"

"We can all feel it," Marshal said. "There is an Inyomere here."

Bennek wondered, "Might it summon the arowl?"

"Maybe. Maybe."

As the darkness deepened, tiny sparks appeared, igniting in the seed heads of the grass, gleaming less than a second, and then vanishing again like stars winking in and out of existence.

Bennek lay wrapped in his blanket, watching the sparks appear and disappear. Within the ground, he began to hear a faint, rhythmic rumbling.

"Listen," Marshal whispered. "Can you hear them? That is the beat of horses' hooves."

Lanyon spoke from out of the darkness. "It's a memory you're hearing. The herds of Samokea used to be vast and beautiful, but they are long gone, prey to the arowl."

Marshal pressed his ear closer to the ground. "I can hear the stallions cry out! I can hear the mares neigh."

"Can you also hear the Inyomere calling?" Bennek asked. "Calling to the horses?"

"I cannot hear him," Kit said. "I can only feel his venom." He shoved his blanket aside and stood to gaze at the sea of grass where the sparks were growing brighter.

Marshal told him, "Put your ear to the ground and you will hear him—though his voice is heartbreaking in its sadness. He cries out, 'Where have you gone?'"

Kit would not listen, but for the others the Inyomere's voice stirred images of the beautiful horses of Samokea, long ago hunted from existence by the ravaging arowl.

"I will listen no more!" Lanyon declared suddenly. She stood up too. "This Inyomere would overwhelm us with his despair."

Kit came to stand beside her. "They hate us." Around them the sparks blazed in the grass, staying longer before winking out. "Why do the Inyomere hate us? Why? It's the arowl that have destroyed the horses, and it was the Inyomere who made the arowl!"

"Siddél made them," Lanyon said. "The other Inyomere did not do this wicked thing."

"The others allowed him to do it. The only purpose of the arowl is to hunt us. The Inyomere do not believe we belong in the Wild."

"They are not like the people," Lanyon conceded. "They are the storms and the seasons, the streams and the glades. They don't understand justice. It's only the Wild they love."

Bennek, too, stood up, to stare pensively into the night.

The sparks had turned into tiny flames that charred the tips of the grass before burning out. They twinkled far out on the prairie and across the river.

"Sometimes I dream of the blessed islands of Hahví," Lanyon said, naming the people's ancestral home. "I don't know if these dreams are true visions or just the echo of stories I've heard, but they are sweet dreams. How I wish I had lived and died then, in the time before the storm."

"So do we all," Kit said reverently.

How the people first came to Hahví, or how long their ancestors had inhabited those kindly islands, no history remembered, but all stories of Hahví were sweet. The Inyomere of those islands had been different from the Inyomere of the Wild. They'd doted on the people, teaching them the crafts it was proper for them to know: writing, so that they might speak to one another from afar and across time, metalwork and architecture, and sea craft, so they could sail from island to island and know all their kin.

But a great storm swept over Hahví. It broke the world and carried away all the Inyomere. Without them, the islands and the sea all around became lifeless and forlorn.

The people had no choice but to flee in their ships. Jahallon had been a youth then. He'd been among the first to set foot on the shore of the Wild.

"Do you think the good Inyomere of those days will ever come back for us?" Bennek wondered.

Lanyon said, "I do not think that could ever be. We are not the same people. We've been stained by this evil we've fought for so long. I don't think the Inyomere of the islands would cherish us as they once did. Perhaps they wouldn't know us at all."

Suddenly the little flames—that before had been so transitory—seemed unwilling to die away. The seed heads burned and it was as if ten thousand candles had been lit at once in the prairie around them. Sparks cascaded to the ground, and in seconds the grass was alight with fitful orange flames.

At first no one could believe it. Siddél was an Inyomere of great power and open malice, but the petty Inyomere—those of the plains, the groves, the streams, the valleys, and the hills—their malice had always been subtle.

Bennek was the first to realize their peril. "Into the stream!" he shouted as the fire found its voice and began to roar. "Grab the gear!"

Kit seized the packs as flames leaped above their heads. Sudden whirlwinds sent pillars of smoke swirling over the faces of the stars. And Lanyon cried out, "Where is Marshal?"

The grass they had trodden flat was already black and smoking. If Marshal still lay there, Bennek could not see him against the glare of orange flame. He bent double and groped in the murk, calling out, "Marshal! Marshal, where have you gone?" Finally, he stumbled against his brother. "Marshal, wake up! Wake up!"

But Marshal lay entranced by the Inyomere's spell. He did not stir.

Kit abandoned the packs. "Come Bennek! We'll drag him to the water."

Too late! The tall flames had swept around them, cutting them off from the stream, confining them in a ring of appalling heat. "We can't get out!" Bennek cried.

As if in answer, a loud barking started up, not far away. Bennek stood to look.

Across the water, a huge dog came running, darting between the spreading flames. A man followed behind the dog, racing past the fires, toward the stream.

Yet the man didn't seem to truly exist. He flickered, appearing and disappearing as he ran, his existence as transient and relentless as a licking flame. In the glaring light Bennek could make out no details of his features, but what did it matter? What else could such a fantastical creature be but the Inyomere who had fired the grass, now caught in the storm of his own anger?

Bennek turned away, and with Kit he lifted Marshal from the smoking ground.

Lanyon stood at the center of their circle, her face lifted to the starry sky. In a voice not her own she spoke a single word—"*Grathrak!*—that somehow carried the ponderous weight of storm clouds.

All across the prairie the flames collapsed as if a giant hand had snuffed them to smoldering ash.

# 7

Bennek could see nothing. His eyes—dazzled by firelight—were blind in a darkness made worse by the choking smoke. But he didn't need sight to feel Marshal wake into life. He set his brother's feet on the ground and, together with Kit, helped him to stand.

Kit asked in a tense voice, "Marshal? Are you all right?"

Marshal swayed. Bennek tightened his grip—then felt his brother tense.

"*Lanyon!*" Marshal cried.

He broke from Bennek and lunged into darkness. There came a soft grunt; the rustle of cloth.

"What's happening?" Bennek whispered.

Marshal answered him, "She's collapsed. I've caught her."

A breeze stirred, carrying some of the smoke away, revealing Marshal's shape as he huddled close to the ground. "She's breathing."

"What's wrong with her?" Kit asked.

"I don't know."

Bennek wanted to go to her, but he groped for his bow instead. They were not out of trouble yet. The Inyomere might have some other wickedness to turn against them. Setting an arrow to his bowstring, he stepped toward the stream.

As the smoke cleared, the stars shone brighter. At the same

time, Bennek's eyes adapted again to the night—and he saw his target.

The Inyomere stood knee-deep in the stream, his figure visible against the reflected starlight glittering in the water. He was bent over, hands propped against knees, and his shoulders heaving as he gasped for air. But when Bennek blinked, the spirit vanished.

Then, after a few pounding heartbeats, the Inyomere appeared again, in the same place but standing upright now, looking at him. A moment later he faded. He did not disappear completely this time, but Bennek could see the glitter of starlight on water through his nebulous shape.

Was the spirit wearing leather armor? Was there a silver tint to his hair? In truth, this being did not look much like an Inyomere. That is, when he looked like anything at all.

The dog didn't suffer its master's affliction of transience. Standing in mid-stream, chest-deep in the sparkling water, it looked as solid as any natural creature of the Wild.

"Stand fast, sir!" Bennek warned, drawing his bow. At the sound of his voice the dog lunged toward him, bounding through the shallow water. "Sir! Calm your dog!"

"Kina, stay! Stay down!" And by speaking, the strange being anchored itself in the world, becoming a solid shadow.

Surely this was a man?

The great hound obeyed her master's command, stopping just short of the bank, but she trembled, thumping her tail against the water and cavorting in place as if overtaken by an intense joy.

"Kina is eager to greet the sorceress," the man said. "Lanyon spoiled her and won her affection."

"You know Lanyon?"

"Jahallon left her in my care"—he coughed hard amid a fresh swirl of smoke—"but I have failed in that."

"You know Jahallon?"

"Son, please put aside your bow before that arrow takes flight on its own."

Marshal stepped up beside him. "Bennek, we do not war against the people."

Bennek lowered his bow. "I apologize, sir. I was startled and fearful, and I mistook you for that Inyomere who ignited the fire."

The stranger's gravelly voice held a hint of amusement. "In all my long years I have never been mistaken for an Inyomere, but then I have also never seen a field set itself on fire. No apology is necessary, sir. Indeed, you have my praise for your alert defense. May I cross the stream?"

"Come over, sir," Marshal said. "The air is better on this side."

His name was Pantheren—a broad-shouldered man of moderate height, with silver hair cropped close to his head in the manner common to the men of Habaddon, and a few days' growth of beard. Even in the darkness, Bennek could see the lines of age upon his face—or he could see them sometimes.

Pantheren still had an element of transience about him. When he stayed still for several seconds, he began to fade, becoming solid again only when he moved or spoke. But it was not the time to question him on it, not when Lanyon lay like one who has been mortally wounded.

Kit held her in his lap, cradling her head in the crook of his arm, while Marshal crouched beside him.

"She still breathes," Kit said in a fearful voice, "but she won't waken."

Pantheren knelt to look at her, and Kina the hound looked too, her head lowered as she gazed mournfully on her friend. Kina was a beautiful dog, her tall, lean body well-balanced, her eyes dark and wide, and her coat a shimmering light gray, just visible in the night.

"Tell me what happened," Pantheren said.

Kit shook his head. "I can't. All I know is the fire went out."

"And I was entranced by the spell of the Inyomere," Marshal said. "I was aware of nothing until she fell."

"I know what happened," Bennek told them. All three looked up at him. "She spoke a word, in a voice that was low and harsh, like something wicked. Then the flames collapsed. Marshal awoke and she fell."

Pantheren sighed and stood again. "It's not without cost that we toy with the arts of the Inyomere."

"She had no choice in it," Bennek said. "The flames were upon us."

"Yet it has proven too much for her."

"She'll come back to us."

Bennek dampened a cloth in the clean water of the stream. Returning to Lanyon, he used it to wipe her face. She *had* to come back.

He thought about how it felt when he hunted with his spirit sight and reached out farther than he should . . . as if he might go on forever, falling away from all he knew. "I will look for her," he announced.

He settled cross-legged on the ground beside her.

"Bennek, wait," Marshal urged, sounding worried.

But Bennek closed his eyes anyway and slipped into the spirit-world, hunting for Lanyon like he hunted the arowl. His ghost-self glided outward, across the grass, past the stream . . . into an empty night. No arowl anywhere, and nothing else that he could discern. He went on anyway, spiraling outward in a widening circle, seeking for her until he felt himself on the verge of falling away into darkness.

*Lanyon!* he thought. *Where are you?*

To his astonishment, she answered: *Bennek!*

Like that time by the river, her voice spoke within his mind, but now sharp with fear.

He answered her with an intensity of thought: *Tell me where you are. I can't see you anywhere.*

*Turn*, she pleaded. *Turn and see me.*

He lurched toward her voice, in a direction that was not north or south, east or west, up or down. It was a turn within—one step that plunged him along a tight, coiled path—and his spirit slipped beneath the world.

He found her there, so close she was almost inside him, as if her shape and his could stand in the same place.

*Take me back*, she pleaded. *I've lost my way.*

She was not alone in that place. Everywhere Bennek looked, he saw the faint, luminous fogs of coy spirits at play, while across the dark fields he saw Marshal, Kit, and Pantheren, all three gilded with radiant life so that the night could not hide them from his vision.

These things he only glimpsed before his attention fixed on a dreadful dark spirit aboil in some deeper place. He feared it at once, but it tantalized him too. It stirred his desire. It tempted him to reach out and possess it, for in possession his fear would surely turn inside out and he would become that which was fearful and dark, and the fear he felt would belong to others.

But Lanyon whispered to him, *It is an evil thing.*

Through her words he remembered himself and his purpose. With ghostly arms, he reached for her. *Hold to me, Lanyon. I'll take you back.*

With her secure in his arms, he turned into himself, and a moment later he opened his eyes and looked at her.

She still rested in Kit's arms, but now starlight glittered in her eyes. "Are you all right, Lanyon?"

She answered with a question of her own. "How did you learn to get to that place, Bennek?"

"I only followed your voice."

"You have not been there before?"

"No. What was that place?"

She said, "It was the Mere."

Then Bennek was all astonishment, for the Mere was the soul of the world. It wound within the ground and within the forests. It surrounded the sky and filled the stones of the mountains. It roared within the ocean and flowed with the waters of rushing streams. It was the lake in which all things floated, and the source from which the Inyomere drew their power. They would sometimes call it the Expanse, but among the people it was more often named the Fourth Way.

It was the place where prayers were sent.

With Kit's assistance, Lanyon sat up. Only then did she notice Pantheren, and her expression hardened. "War Father! When the mist spoke her warning, I knew it was you she meant. Sir, I will not go to Habaddon!"

"I have given up all hope of persuading you to that, Lanyon Kyramanthes."

"Then why have you followed me? You could have returned safely to Jahallon."

"Jahallon made it my duty to look after you. Not until I met you have I ever failed in my duty. Do you still have the talisman?"

Lanyon touched the strap that held the bundled arrow. "I have it."

Bennek asked, "Is that the dark presence I saw within the Mere?"

She nodded. "It *is* an evil thing."

Pantheren turned to Marshal. "Though we didn't meet, I remember you and your kin from Habaddon. There was much discussion of the Samokeän boys among the captains. We could see you were battle-worthy and any of us would have been pleased to accept your oath, but Jahallon wouldn't allow it."

This stunned them, for though the men of Habaddon had been friendly, they had offered no encouragement.

"They mistrusted our experience," Marshal said, "and advised us to train another year."

"Is that what you were told? Jahallon's words were somewhat different. He said you should have another season in the world. I thought it only a whim of his, but Jahallon has foresight, and now I must wonder if he knew there was another path for you."

"It was not Jahallon's will that summoned us north," Bennek said. "We were called by the Snow Chanter. She awaits us."

"Indeed?"

"We dream of her every night," Marshal said as he recovered his pack from the darkness. "Though this night I think we should forego sleep and move on, for the smoke is choking and I cannot sleep amid the ash."

All agreed. They gathered their packs and weapons, and filled their water skins. Kina walked among them, a great, menacing shape in the darkness. Bennek watched her sidelong. His father had kept a war dog—so he had been told—but like his father it had not returned from battle.

"*Kina.*" He whispered her name as she passed near him and she turned to look. He couldn't see her expression in the darkness, but when he raised a tentative hand she came to snuffle his scent. Moving with great caution, he touched her head—her fur was so much softer than he had imagined!—but he snatched his hand back when a shadow loomed beside him.

"Don't be nervous," Lanyon said softly.

"I don't know much about dogs."

"Stroke her like this." She demonstrated. "Or scratch her behind her ears." Bennek tried it, and Kina wagged her tail with pleasure.

Lanyon turned to look for Pantheren. "War Father, where is your sweet mare?"

Pantheren answered from the darkness. "I set her free, with her nose pointed to Habaddon. Perhaps she will find her way back. If I had brought her farther into Samokea, her warm flesh would have drawn the arowl within hours."

They set out again across the wide prairie. Kina the hound went first, for the night was nothing to her. She led them around stones, animal burrows, and dry streambeds. Near midnight they found another running stream and there Marshal called a halt. Bennek trampled down a circle of grass and dropped his pack. "It might be the same place as before—except I am even hungrier."

"We'll find something to eat tomorrow," Marshal told him.

"Hunting is easy," Kit said. "But how can we cook in this treeless land?"

Pantheren rummaged in his pack, pulling out a cloth-wrapped bundle. "I cannot conjure a fire for you, but I can ease your stomachs tonight. When Lanyon abandoned me, she left me by far the greatest share of food."

He opened the bundle to reveal flatbread, smoked fish, and dried fruit. The Samokeän boys accepted it all gratefully, and their spirits rose as they ate.

Just as they finished, Bennek heard a rustle in the grass behind him. He leaped to his feet, heart pounding, and drew his sword. But it was only Kina, returning from the grass with a pleased look, her tongue lolling.

"She hunts her own food," Pantheren said with a flash of white teeth that must have been a grin.

After Bennek put his sword away, Kina came to sniff his hands and he smiled, wondering how she'd guessed he had saved a bit of bread for her. She took the gift with great dignity. Then she went to lie down near Pantheren.

Marshal spoke. "War Father, you are a hard man to see. You fade from sight altogether whenever you're still. It's as if you've been protected by Lanyon's spell of the Hunter's Veil, though with you, it endures."

"It is indeed Lanyon's doing. A gift from her when she abandoned me. She wrapped me in a veiling spell and sent me into an unnatural sleep. Only by the stars do I know that two nights passed." He held out his hands. At first they were visible in the starlight, but then they faded from sight. "The enchantment clings."

"Lanyon," Bennek asked, "is this the same spell of concealment you put on us when we hunted the arowl?"

She had been silent since they left the burned fields. Now she answered quietly, "That was less powerful, for there was less time."

Marshal asked, "Was it you, sir, in the cane beside the River Talahnon?"

"Yes, that was me. I wanted to understand Lanyon's intentions before I showed myself to her again."

"I told you my intentions," she said, an edge to her voice. "I told you of the arrow. I told you where I was bound."

"But you did not tell these things to Jahallon! You let him believe we would go to Habaddon."

"He would have stopped me if he knew!"

"He *is* your far father!"

"He does not see all things!"

The Samokeän boys were astonished at the sudden heat of this quarrel. Marshal spoke in a gentle voice, determined to diffuse it. "We too left Habaddon in deceit. We let our friends believe we were returning to Fathalia. Sometimes those who love us protect us too much."

Kit looked at Pantheren and cocked his head. "Do you think it is a mad task to seek to slay Siddél?"

"Without hope of success," Pantheren assured him.

"Neither is there hope in this endless war," Lanyon countered. "The arowl cannot be defeated while Siddél lives to conjure ever more of their kind."

Marshal told Pantheren, "We've promised Lanyon our aid after we find the Snow Chanter. We'll go with her to the Storm Lair, and there we'll lie in wait for Siddél."

"It's a worthy task," Kit added, "if even Jahallon's captain would refuse it."

Pantheren chuckled in the darkness. "There was talk in Habaddon that you Samokeän boys were somewhat addled by the hardship of your lives, but blessed, too, for you still owned them."

A shocked silence descended on their circle. Kit started to rise.

"Stay, son," Pantheren said with humor in his voice. "Even if true, there is no insult in it. It only means you are brave and lucky, and—perhaps—fated. I know my fate has come down on me." He turned to Lanyon. "I will not fight you anymore, Lanyon Kyramanthes. If this is the task you have chosen, then I'll help you in it as I can."

"Though you don't believe in it?"

"Not so many days ago I would not have believed in you. For now, I'll put belief aside."

It was ever Bennek's duty to keep the last watch before sunrise. He stood away from the camp, leaning on his spear, facing into the wind that hissed through the tall grass. Sometimes on watch he would census the stars, his lips moving as he recited their names in a soundless chant. Other times he would listen to the rustles and calls of little animals engaged in their nightly tasks, and by morning he would know their kind, and where their burrows and nests must be.

On that night though, his thoughts turned to his fleeting visit to the Mere. The memory preoccupied him. He longed to know if he could find his way back there again. He thought he could.

All was silent. Nothing was about. No harm could come if he spent some part of his watch in that way peculiar to him. So, still leaning on his spear, he closed his eyes and allowed his ghost-self to drift free. He did not seek the arowl. There were none around. Instead, he sought to remember the sound of Lanyon's voice and the direction from which it had come. It had been a direction he had never imagined before, not up or down, forward or back, left or right... but a Fourth Way. He turned toward the memory, and once again he slipped beneath the world.

Stars still filled the night sky, and tall grass still swayed upon the land. Yet this was only the surface of things. Beneath, within, at the center, there existed a heaving, frothing, flowing vastness of indifferent awareness—the Mere—where brooding forces dwelled, enduring a slow decay. Bennek felt himself diminished in the face of it. With a shudder he turned away, feeling safe only on the margin.

He found his vision sharpened. When he gazed toward the camp he saw Kit and Marshal and Pantheren there all asleep. They should have been hidden from him by darkness and by the tall grass, yet they gleamed in his awareness, not as light is usually perceived, but with a luminous gravity irresistible to his gaze. Never before in his forays through the spirit-world had he been so aware of the presence of people.

He sensed another being too, though its gravity was shifting and fickle. It was not the talisman. That wicked presence was a separate thing. This other was coy, like a gleam of light in the corner of his eye, retreating from view even as he turned to see it, leaving him uncertain if it was there at all.

After a few minutes, he set aside this puzzle and sent his ghost-self forth, into the camp. There he discovered Kina asleep near her master. To his surprise, he found her presence faint, and hard to perceive.

Then he noticed what he had overlooked before: Lanyon was not there. He saw only trammeled grass where she'd been sleeping. With his spirit sight he searched for her on the prairie, but he could not find her. It was as if she'd vanished from the world.

Fear took him. He returned to himself and then raced back to camp. Pantheren and Marshal heard him coming. They awaited him, weapons in hand, when he lunged into the circle of flattened grass. "Where is Lanyon?" he cried, as Kit too abandoned sleep. "She has disappeared!"

But there she was, sitting up in the starlight. "Bennek?"

He stared at her in confusion. "Where were you?"

"Here! Just as you see me now."

"But I couldn't see you at all! You were gone."

"No. I've gone nowhere. It's just that it's dark. I'm wearing black, and—"

"I was within the Mere. My sight was untroubled by darkness. I could see each stem of bent grass, but Lanyon, you were nowhere to be found."

"Oh." She glanced at Pantheren as he laid down his sword. "It would be dangerous for me if I let myself be seen within the Mere."

"You mean you've hidden yourself?" The possibility both surprised and troubled Bennek. It made him a little angry too, to learn that the clarity of the Mere was an illusion, and that he had been misled.

Lanyon nodded. "It's a skill of the Inyomere, to weave a glamour that will lead the eye away."

"And you know how to do it . . . so you are hidden from Siddél?"

"I hope I am hidden from all who see within the Mere."

"Truly, there must be many among the Inyomere who would stop you if they knew what you intend."

"I just wish I could hide the talisman too, but I don't know how to do that."

Bennek wondered if he had been foolish. But how could he have known? He knew so little.

He apologized for waking everyone. Then he returned to his watch. He did not wander again that night.

# 8

THE DAY DAWNED clear and cool, though the air warmed quickly once the sun rose. They set out early and by noon they had covered many miles. They still saw no trees, but Lanyon discovered a stream with sticks of driftwood scattered on its banks. "Let's make a meal here while we may."

"We haven't hunted," Kit said.

"There are fish in the stream. I will get some. They cook faster than birds or rabbits anyway. Make a fire. It will take me only a few minutes."

"It's best to acquiesce," Pantheren advised, stooping to pick up a piece of wood. "I assure you nothing will be achieved by argument."

"How will you get the fish?" Bennek wondered, following Lanyon down to the water. "I had meant to ask how you had done it before."

She set down her bundles. "I've been able to catch fish since I was a little girl. My mother showed me how."

She startled him by pulling off her long black robe. Underneath she was dressed in a black tunic and in black leather pants. She rolled up her pants until her legs were bare to the knee. Then she took off her shoes and waded into the water.

She said, "It's a simple thing. You face upstream. Then you call the fish with your thoughts."

Her voice grew softer. "Bennek, I have not thanked you for bringing me back when I became lost in the deep places of the Mere. It was all aboil about me, and I didn't know which way to turn until you came."

"Why did you become lost?"

"I was pulled under by the spell whose name I spoke." She trailed her hand in the cold water that sluiced past her knees. "It was an Inyomere's spell, and much stronger than I am. I should not have called on it, but I didn't know what else to do. I am grateful you summoned me back, and I thank you." Then she smiled, and when she spoke again, her voice was merry. "It's only a small step to summoning fish! You might be able to learn, though in Clan Kyramanthes it was only the women who fished."

"Show me then."

She leaned forward, staring intently at the stream's rippling surface. Before long, her hands plunged into the water and up came a silvery fish that did not flap or wriggle.

"It's stunned!" Bennek objected, as if this meant she was cheating.

She lobbed it at him and he laughed, jumping aside. "If you will not gather wood, then clean the fish," she commanded.

"As you wish, ma'am."

They set out again in the afternoon. Near evening the wind turned. It swept away a haze they had hardly been aware of. A chain of snow-capped mountains stood revealed to the west, surprisingly close, rising abruptly from the rolling green grasslands of Samokea.

The boys gazed at the peaks in astonishment.

"The Tiyat-kel!" Bennek said. He turned to Marshal and Kit. "The Snow Chanter is there. Can you feel it?"

Kit nodded. "These are the very peaks I've seen in my dreams."

"I can see the way in my mind," Marshal agreed. "Yet the day's light is fading. We must be content to camp one more night in the grasslands. But tomorrow we'll reach the mountains."

———

In that region, the streams that ran down from the Tiyat-kel had cut shallow gullies in the prairie. Thickets grew within them, yielding an abundance of fallen wood, so that evening they enjoyed a fire.

Pantheren opened his pack, and from it he took a folded wallet that held an awl, an artisan's knife, and a small wooden block. Next he unfolded a strap of fine, thin leather. It was the width of his palm and as long as his spear, deep red in color, and half its length was inscribed with finely shaped characters in the script taught to the people long ago by the good Inyomere of Hahví.

The characters had been made by carving away the red surface of the leather, exposing the white inner layer. They spoke the traditional prayers: of gratitude for the beneficence of the Wild, of devotion to its renewal, and of wrath and reprisal against the arowl. The firelight shone through the script, and the wind swept past it, both powers carrying the prayers into the Mere.

Pantheren sat close to the firelight and, placing the wooden block beneath the leather strap, he began to add new lines to the prayer ribbon.

Bennek watched him curiously. He had seen such things in Habaddon, but had only ever been taught to carve the prayers on leaves or the inner side of bark, which would then go into the fire. After a while, it seemed to him the symbols wrote themselves onto the prayer banner, for Pantheren did not appear to be there anymore.

"Lanyon," Bennek wondered, "how long will your Hunter's Veil cling to Pantheren?"

She sat on the edge of the firelight, working the rabbit skins, stretching and pulling them over a smooth stone to make them supple. "I don't know."

He laughed. "How can you not know?"

"But how could I? I called the spell many, many times—more than I ever have before—until it was strong. I wanted it to last until Pantheren reached the Glycian. I meant for him to return to Habaddon, not follow after me."

At this, Pantheren made a dismissive *harrumph*, but Bennek wanted to know more. "Is there a way to undo the enchantment?"

"Oh yes," she said in humor, "but Pantheren is safer thus."

Pantheren answered this sharply—"It's your safety that matters, Lanyon Kyramanthes, not mine"—and by his words he was made visible again, sitting bent over the prayer ribbon, carefully working the lines of a complex symbol. "You would do well to use your skills to hide yourself."

"My skills are slight. I have not the strength to walk always in veils."

"You called the fire spell," Bennek countered. "You armed Pantheren with an enchantment that has endured for days. You crushed a grass fire with a single word. If such skills are deemed slight in Ohtangia, your people must have been great sorcerers. How can it be they didn't thrive?"

All waited for her answer. Even Pantheren ceased working on his prayer ribbon. She traded a look with him. Then she turned to Bennek. "I learned these skills in Samokea."

He started to smile, but thought better of it when he saw the glint in her eye. "I don't understand you."

"I learned these skills from Édan, who was my husband."

This claim stunned Bennek into silence. How could it be true? Édan had lived and died long, long ago. He could not have been her husband. It was impossible.

Lanyon said, "You don't want to believe me, but it is true."

"*How* is it true? Unless you are of the Inyomere? Or have you been bound to this world like Jahallon?"

Bennek had only spoken aloud his own racing thoughts. He had not meant to frighten her. But wide-eyed fear displaced her determined expression. She turned to Pantheren, and asked in a trembling voice, "War Father, could it be so? Have I been cursed as Jahallon is cursed?"

"No! You are here because your spell let you slip through time."

Bennek realized she had never considered such a doom before, and he desperately wished he could take back his words. "Lanyon, please. Do not listen to me. Of course it can't be true."

The rabbit skin fell from her shaking hands. "I did not mean for it to happen this way! Édan was dead and our children before him, but Siddél was still in the keep and all was afire. I didn't want to die in the fire! So I called a spell to bridge the moments. To step outside of time for some small while . . . a chance for the monster to depart, for the fire to pass me by . . . but with the arrow in my hands the spell became something more."

She looked at her shaking hands, turning them over in the firelight. "I left the world on that night. I don't know where I went. It was like being on the edge of some vague, sweet dream. I know that time passed. My heart healed. Jahallon says it is 137 years since the Citadel fell." She shook her head. "I only know that when I returned I was no older, but everything around me lay in cold ruin.

"I was still within the Citadel of the Snow Chanter, but the walls and towers were fallen and the land was dead, its life all consumed. The wind blew, fierce and cold and full of dust. It wailed with the lamentation of the Inyomere—all those spirits who had lost their forests and meadows, their streams and ponds, all the creatures of their lands, all of it, forever gone away . . . even the arowl pits of Siddél had been left dead and empty."

She touched a hand to her chest. "I thought some final calamity had befallen the Wild, that it had been forsaken by the One. There was nothing to eat. Nothing to drink. For days I ventured south and there was nothing! War Father, Bennek is right. I should have died."

"I did not say that!" Bennek protested.

Pantheren spoke to her in a voice both calm and firm. "You're not like Jahallon. You would know it if you were. Jahallon knew. You're stronger than you think, and perhaps there's an effect from Édan's arrow, so that it sustains you."

"It must be that," Bennek said quickly. He went to her. He knelt beside her and took her hand. "Lanyon, please forgive me for frightening you. I speak too quickly. I speak without the least thought. I know it and I'm sorry."

"It's not your fault. And in the end it makes no difference. My task is the same."

There followed gentle questions from Marshal and Kit. They

learned that Jahallon had believed Lanyon among the dead on that night the Citadel of the Snow Chanter was overrun.

Bennek sat beside her, on the edge of the firelight. "I read an account of that night. Jahallon saw the tower in flames. He saw the roof collapse. He believed all within were dead."

"He never doubted her death," Pantheren confirmed. "Not until this summer, when she returned."

The army had been encamped on the outskirts of Nendaganon when Jahallon sensed her return *'like a thunderclap in the Mere.'* Jahallon had called Pantheren to him and they left at once, riding north to find her. "I think, Lanyon, you were as astonished to see us as we were to find you."

"That is true. I saw such devastation. I came to believe I was the last of the people in the Wild."

"Did Édan make the arrow?" Bennek asked. "Did he make it that night?"

Lanyon nodded miserably. "You have seen its spell. It is a dark and fearsome presence in the Mere. Imagine the forces that were stirred when Édan first made it."

Bennek understood. "Siddél would have sensed its creation. So he knew what Édan had done. In the account I read, Siddél was heard to thunder, *'I am come! To see you slain by your own spell.'* Now I know he meant the arrow."

"Yes, and Édan is gone from the world. But the arrow is still here and I will use it to end Siddél's life, just as Édan intended."

# 9

THE NEXT DAY they set out before dawn and by late morning they were only a few miles from the mountains. The highlands rose abruptly out of the plain, standing up behind a towering palisade of gray rock. On the slopes above the cliffs, an amber-leaved forest climbed to a high country of evergreens that in turn gave way to ragged snow fields at the cloud-wrapped summits.

That morning there had been only a light breeze out of the east. But the wind turned, sweeping down from the north in a strong, steady current. Kina the hound had been dividing her time between Pantheren and Bennek, but when the wind changed she loped ahead, stopping on a slight rise, her nose savoring messages carried on the air.

"Hallo girl!" Pantheren called. "What have you found?"

When they caught up with her, they discovered the coarse hair of her neck standing on end. A growl rumbled in her throat, and her lips drew up in a cruel snarl.

"Everyone, get down now!" Pantheren ordered, and such was the urgency in his voice that they all dropped at once below the level of the tall grass, and Kina lay down with them. "She scents arowl."

"We have been inattentive!" Marshal said. "It's been three days since we encountered arowl, but that respite should have made us more vigilant, not less."

Bennek felt the sting of guilt, knowing he had been remiss. His talent was far-seeing, but he had not taken the time to search the land since they had set out in the early morning. Now he suffered the weight of Marshal's gaze.

"I'll see what I can discover," he said quietly. Closing his eyes, he stepped outside himself, then turned in the Fourth Way.

An expansive vision opened to him, yet he discovered no arowl within the reach of his sight. So he extended himself farther, bracing for the dizzying sensation of tumbling away, away from the world . . . but it didn't come. A thread within the Mere bound him to himself, and when he had reached as far as he was able, he simply waited. It was only a little while, when a faint, ugly presence stirred on the edge of his senses.

Marshal waited anxiously for Bennek's verdict. Minutes passed. Then Bennek started to tremble. His breathing quickened. A sheen of sweat appeared on his cheeks. "Bennek," Marshal said, squeezing his brother's shoulder. "Bennek, come back."

Bennek gasped. His eyes opened. "Marshal!"

Marshal had never before seen such fear on his brother's face. Kina, too, sensed his distress. She pushed between them, shoving her head against Bennek's shoulder.

"What did you see?" Marshal demanded.

"Arowl." Bennek stroked the dog with a shaking hand. "Many arowl." His frightened gaze turned north, though from his low vantage he couldn't see anything but grass.

"How many is many?" Kit wanted to know. "Thirty? Fifty?"

Bennek stared at Kit as if he had made a crude joke. His fingers clenched Kina's fur. "No, sir," he whispered. "There are very many more than that."

He turned to Marshal. "There might be two hundred fifty. Maybe three hundred. More. Too many to count. They are still some miles to the north, but running hard toward us." He breathed in quick gasps. A flush heated his cheeks.

Turning to Lanyon, he said, "Can you make a spell to hide us?"

"There is no time!" she answered, her eyes wide with fright.

Marshal, too, felt afraid. His skin prickled. His heart thundered in his ears. But he fixed Bennek with a stern gaze, determined to quash any sign of panic. "Remember your gifts. It's up to you to confound the arowl."

"I cannot confound so many!"

"You will do it if it must be done."

"Do they know we're here?" Pantheren asked. "Bennek, can you tell?"

"They are stampeding toward us! Of course they know."

"Are you sure? Is it us they hunt? Check, Bennek. Confirm it if you can."

"Do it," Marshal commanded.

Still holding onto Kina, Bennek closed his eyes again.

Pantheren said, "The stream we just passed—it had steep banks with overhanging weeds. We'll hide ourselves there."

"We might hide ourselves," Kit agreed with an odd half-smile. "But we can't hide our scent, which has grown somewhat strong of late. It's a shame, War Father, that your own obscurity is finally fading."

"Kit's right," Marshal said. "With so many on the hunt, they will find us."

Pantheren's hard-eyed gaze took them both in. "That may be, but until then, we do all we can. Do not embrace hopelessness."

"I hope to win through to the Snow Chanter," Kit said, with an angry edge to his words. "But if these arowl have been sent by her enemies to stop us, there is no hope in hiding."

Lanyon spoke up, her voice quavering, "Still, we can try. I know a spell that may help hide our tracks, at least."

"Use it," Pantheren told her. "Kit, come with me. Let's go back to the stream and prepare a place."

Kit looked ready to resist, but Marshal told him, "*Go.* It's our best chance."

Kit responded with a hiss, his expression grim and skeptical, but he left with Pantheren.

Marshal stayed with Bennek, along with Lanyon and Kina. After a minute, Bennek opened his eyes again. He blinked. His brow furrowed. He looked both puzzled and anxious.

"Well?" Marshal asked. "What did you discern?"

"I can't tell what they hunt. They run with a desperate speed, though toward what I cannot say. More are coming, from west and east. And there are more still to the south, though these run away from us."

"Then they pursue something else," Lanyon concluded. "They don't know we're here."

Marshal allowed himself to hope. "May it be so. Come. Let's follow Kit and Pantheren. We'll hide as we can."

Kit's mouth turned in a cold half-smile when Bennek shared the news of what he had seen. "I hope this time you have it right, my cousin."

"As do I," Bennek said in full sincerity.

"Let us hold onto hope," Pantheren told them. "But let us hurry. Already I can hear the yammering of the pack. Remember, to hide and do nothing is our best hope, but if you must kill, do it quickly so the beast does not alert its mates."

The stream had steep, crumbling banks nearly four feet high. Spring floods had undercut them, and then over the long summer weeds had grown over them so that now an amber-leaved drapery concealed a collection of dry and tidy hollows.

Kit directed Bennek to crawl into a sheltered place on the north side. "Lie down against the dry bank and get comfortable. No one may move once we've settled." Kit came in behind him, and readied his bow. There was space left only for Marshal, who slipped in next past the weeds.

"What of Lanyon and Pantheren?" Bennek whispered.

Kit said, "They'll take Kina and conceal themselves in another hollow just upstream."

"Now we must be silent," Marshal whispered. "Not a sound from this moment forward."

Bennek gazed past the weeds, worrying over the scuff marks left by their boots in the crumbling soil, but even as he watched, a swirling wind lifted them away.

The howls and barking of the arowl pack could be heard clearly now, carried south on the wind. Bennek listened to the bone-chilling cries and the hair on his neck rose, just as Kina's had. He hoped the dog would lie quietly. He hoped the arowl had other prey in mind—but then he hoped they didn't, for he wouldn't wish this pack on anyone.

A tapping on his thigh made him shift his gaze. Marshal gave him an impatient look, and Bennek nodded. He closed his eyes and again he let his ghost-self step into the Fourth Way.

Suddenly, the yammering and crying of the arowl was no longer distant. They were all around him and he was a wraith, carried south by a strong wind. He shed fear among them, but they did not notice, so fearful were they already. So he urged them to greater speed, hoping to drive them to exhaustion before they reached the streambed, but they could run no faster than they already did.

In the half-light under the bank, Marshal watched his brother, gauging their peril by the tension, the raw fear on Bennek's face.

The crying of the pack drew rapidly nearer. The hard tread of their paws and hooves reverberated in the ground, growing louder and louder as the seconds passed until the pack was upon them.

*Be still*, Marshal thought. *Restrain your fear and move not.* To his pride, neither Kit nor Bennek gave way to panic—even when the first arowl leapt down from the bank, landing with a thud and a splash in the streambed just a few feet from their position.

Marshal had not seen the great dire wolf slain by Bennek, but this was surely the same kind of beast: an immense, reeking, wolfish thing, with diagonal slashes of thin white fur scarring its shoulders. A festering wound on its neck made it easy to see the collar it wore. A remnant chain swung loose at its throat, clanging as the beast bounded across the streambed. It leapt to the top of the southern bank, and raced out of sight.

Three smaller wolfish arowl leaped down into the stream, splashing across it. A panting were-wolf followed.

Next, the ground trembled with heavy footfalls. Part of the bank gave way as a massive were-bear slid into the streambed. The beast stood in the water, its body all too much like that of a huge man but covered in long brown fur. Its head was a wickedly distorted bear's head. Slashes of white fur marked its hairy cheeks. In its thick-fingered hands it held a spear tipped with a stone-blade the length of Marshal's forearm.

The beast jerked its head from side to side, its nostrils flaring suspiciously, searching out a teasing scent. Then it pointed its snout at the sky and uttered a long, forlorn keening—a loathsome sound that no bear of the Wild had ever made.

Marshal felt Kit trembling. Bennek's knuckles had gone white around the shaft of his spear.

The were-bear listened as another of its kind answered its cry from far away. It sniffed the air again and started to swing its head low . . .

Then, abruptly, it jerked upright again, barking in vile syllables. As if instilled with a fresh sense of urgency, it bounded to the southern bank, scrambled up, and loped away.

A few more small arowl passed by. Stragglers, Marshal guessed. The last of the pack. Still, he did not move. He waited, listening, as the howling of the arowl grew gradually fainter, finally fading away altogether, leaving only the hiss of wind in the grass.

"They are gone," Bennek whispered. "They have all gone away south."

Marshal slipped out from the hollow to meet Pantheren by the stream. Kina slunk beside him, leashed and trembling.

"I have never seen or heard of such a migration," Pantheren said. "I fear what it means."

"Do you think they intend an assault on Habaddon?"

"That is the simplest answer, and yet it would take many more arowl than these to threaten our city."

"I'm worried they will turn back to hunt us," Marshal admitted. "Let's go on as quickly as we may."

They followed the stream, and within an hour they reached the great palisade. Marshal gazed up at it. "I know this place. I've seen it in my dreams."

The cliff loomed above him, smooth and sheer. It appeared

impossible to climb. But Marshal knew the way. "Come," he said, leading them north. "There's a break in the wall not far from here."

His prescience proved true. The wall had been fractured in some ancient cataclysm, creating a narrow fissure that they could climb—though it proved to be an exhausting ascent. Dense, brittle thickets covered the precipitous slope, forcing them to break their own path. And they were miserably hot because the north wind could not get into the crevice, and the narrow rock walls redoubled the heat of the sun.

Through the whole long climb, Marshal could not see what transpired on the plain, except for a narrow vista looking east—but there, at least, he saw no more arowl.

The afternoon was half-gone by the time they reached the top of the palisade. Lanyon had removed her black robe during the climb, but as they left the shelter of the fissure, the powerful north wind swept down on them, and she quickly put it on again.

They rested a few minutes and shared a small meal, all the while watching the prairie below, but no arowl moved there, nor anything larger than a soaring pheasant.

They went on, climbing through a forest bright with autumn colors, until in the evening they came on a little valley nestled among peaks. Here they decided to make their camp.

Lanyon stayed up late to sew the rabbit hide into shoes, and Pantheren helped her in this task. So they were still awake when Kit stirred, rising in the middle night to take the watch as was his custom. His eyes glistened in the fire's ruddy light. "I have dreamed of the Snow Chanter," he whispered. "She knows we have come."

Lanyon looked on him in wonder. "You've seen the way to her?"

"She is at the summit of this mountain, trapped within ice, but the way is perilous." He said this with a smile as if it pleased him. "Still, if the goats may climb there, we can too."

# 10

In the morning, Marshal described the same dream as Kit, and all were eager to seek the path to the summit.

They set out as soon as they could, hiking swiftly to the back of the valley, where they encountered a great gray cliff like a second palisade, rising a thousand feet or more before disappearing into gray, swirling clouds.

Goats lived on this cliff, their shaggy coats charcoal gray like the stone. None bleated, for such sounds would draw the arowl. When the goats noticed people below them, they retreated silently upward. Pantheren watched them climb, then turned a doubtful eye on Kit. "You are sure this is the way?"

Kit grinned. "War Father, do you hesitate?"

Pantheren made a rumbling noise deep in his throat. "You will not find many foolhardy *old* men in the world."

"The way will be difficult," Marshal admitted. "But I think not as bad as it looks. We have only to follow the goat paths."

"I cannot see any paths," Lanyon said quietly.

To Bennek's eye, she looked a little queasy. He touched her hand. "I'll help you climb." His sleep had been too deep for dreaming, but the heights did not daunt him, and he wanted to make the most of the day. "It won't be long before we reach the top and with luck we'll find the Snow Chanter before darkness falls."

Kit set out first to scout a way. He found goat paths scuffed and scarred by hooves, and marked with dung. The paths took them up steep inclines, across narrow ledges, and through deep grooves that wound up the rock face.

Marshal followed behind Kit, though his gaze was as often on the valley as on the rocks ahead. He worried an arowl pack would discover their trail.

Kina went after him, trembling and uncertain in places, but in others jumping boldly over crevices that the people would cross only with great care. Pantheren followed behind the hound, encouraging her in narrow places, and helping Lanyon, who came after him. Bennek came last, his calm confidence fortifying Lanyon against the terror of the heights.

They climbed steadily, encouraging one another, aware always of the dizzying gulf of air only a misstep away. And whenever they could, they helped each other. At the worst parts one would cross, then turn and reach a hand back for the next.

"I shall dream of heights forever," Lanyon whispered when they rested at mid-morning, perched in an aerie of rock far above the valley floor. "I think I would have made a very unhappy bird."

Pantheren grunted. "If I were a bird, I would be a partridge crouched beneath thickets."

Kit laughed and threw a stone off the cliff face. It seemed to fall forever. "If I had to be a bird, I would be a hawk and spy out the arowl for the people."

"It's sad birds don't help us in this way," Bennek mused. "Then again, it's not their task to care for the Wild."

Near noon, they reached the top of the escarpment. They found themselves in a wide mountain pass carpeted in golden heath and fenced north and south by gray peaks frosted with snow.

Marshal, Kit, and Bennek took counsel together. All felt the will of the Snow Chanter, drawing them on to a place of ice and deadly cold.

"I'm sure of this much," Marshal said. "We must seek the far end of this pass."

They set out again, making good time through the heath, and by midafternoon they had traversed the pass, and reached the western side of the mountains. Here they looked down a long slope of loose gray stone that ended abruptly a half mile below them, as if at another precipice.

Far beyond that, they could see a vast, brown lowland reaching to the horizon. Dark pits scarred its face, softened only a little by a haze of blowing dust. Nowhere in that expanse did they see the hopeful green of trees or grass. Nowhere the blue of water.

A stiff wind plucked at the fabric of Lanyon's robe as she said, "Behold the arowl pits of Siddél. The monster would destroy the Wild, rather than let us live in it."

"Look to the north," Marshal urged them. "Through the haze, just on the edge of sight. Those are mountains running west. Surely they are the Armory Peaks that we saw on the maps?"

"Indeed," Pantheren said. "Among those peaks were the iron quarries of Samoket. Now we know just how far north we have come."

Lanyon turned away from the precipice, hugging herself against the cold blast of the wind. "Where now shall we go?"

Even as she asked the question, she looked up at the northern heights and found her answer. Two peaks could now be seen, that had not been visible from within the pass. A white cliff filled the high saddle between them, its face so blindingly bright in the sunlight Lanyon knew it was not stone at all, but ice. More ice lay below it in an apron nestled between the slopes.

"The Snow Chanter is there," she announced, as the knowledge washed over her with the certainty of enchantment. "Marshal, turn and look. Tell me, do you feel it too?"

Marshal's eyes went wide. Bennek and Kit confirmed it.

"We have found her," Kit said. "But we must hurry, for the day is passing."

Kit set a blistering pace, and by late afternoon they reached the crumbling edge of the ice field.

Over the summer the ice had eroded, so that it stood in fantastic towers and crumbling arches that caught fire in the lowering sun. Melt water ran from it in a net of dripping, trickling, gushing streamlets that made a bog of the approach.

They climbed the gray rocks alongside the frozen field. Bennek felt the near presence of the Snow Chanter, and yet she was not near enough. They climbed higher. The ice field grew wider as they ascended until after half an hour they looked out across a vast labyrinth of pinnacles and crevices, all agleam with the orange glow of the descending sun.

Marshal called a halt. He stood with eyes half closed, as if listening. "She is here. So close, I can almost hear her heart beating."

He shrugged off his pack, and then he laid his bow beside it. Bennek and Kit did the same. Carrying only their swords, they set out across the ice, slipping and skidding, catching themselves with their hands. Only the unlined leather of their bowman's gloves protected their palms from the cold.

Pantheren called Kina and leashed her to the packs. "I will not have her break a leg," he told Lanyon, who was putting on her new shoes, pulling them on over her old ones, the better to keep her feet warm. "Wait here until we find something."

"I cannot. I promised I would help them in their quest."

She followed Pantheren, leaving Kina to whine at the indignity of being left behind.

They wandered among spires, crevices, caves, and glistening arches, pursuing the presence of the Snow Chanter. But in the labyrinth of the ice she seemed to be everywhere and nowhere: the sense of her presence mirrored in every glassy surface, a thousand reflections of her gravity and none of them the true source.

Marshal could not say which way was the right way to find the frozen prison where she lay entombed. Kit could not sense the path that would lead to her. Bennek felt her presence as a fierce desire for freedom seeping up from the ice, inconstant, deceptive, pulling him in a hundred different directions that led nowhere.

As time passed, their hands and feet went icy and numb. Pantheren gave Lanyon his gloves to wear, but even so her fingers became so cold and stiff she could hardly move them. Now the sun was nearing the horizon. Marshal watched in despair as its rim struck the edge of the world.

"We have tomorrow," Pantheren said gently. "New hope may rise with the sun."

"We must find her!" Bennek insisted. "We can't fail now."

But the day's end had come. The sun passed from the Wild. Bitter cold descended on them so that even Marshal began to shiver. "Let's find some wood," he said, "and make a camp before the light fails."

Moving in a glum line, they made their way back toward the packs. Bennek went last, trailing behind Lanyon. Every few steps he paused to gaze again across the ice. So it was that he saw gray movement to the north, where the twilight reflected from the ice in cool hues. Something was moving in the labyrinth, silent and fleet. Not arowl. No arowl could be so quiet.

He clambered up a pedestal of ice to get a better look, but he took one step too far. The ice underneath him shattered. He cried out, plunging and sliding fifteen feet or more into a fissure, where he struck bottom, hard. Shards of falling ice crashed around him. He rolled over and covered his head until it stopped. Then he sat up slowly, wincing at his bruised back and side.

A deep twilight surrounded him. There was just enough light to make out an uneven floor, like scar tissue forming as the ice split apart. Smooth blue walls towered on either side, rising to a fragile roof of white ice with a hole broken in it where he had fallen through. Standing up, Bennek unsheathed his knife. He would not be climbing out until he cut steps.

"Bennek?" Lanyon's frantic cry reached him from a distance. "Bennek, what happened? Where are you?"

"I'm here, Lanyon. I fell through the ice."

"I hear you! But I don't know where you are."

Again, gray movement caught his eye. He looked around, the knife ready in his hand.

Within the fissure, not a spear's length away, sat a great snow leopard watching him, its blue eyes faintly luminous in the shadows. It was a strikingly beautiful creature, its long white fur marked with charcoal half circles.

"Hallo," he called softly.

The cat slipped soundlessly round a bend in the fissure and out of sight. Cautiously, Bennek followed after it. Peering around the bend, he discovered a small, slender woman standing there, not four feet tall, dressed in a robe of snow leopard fur. She had long white hair and blue eyes that gleamed bright with their own light.

Bennek knew without doubt that she was the Inyomere of this place: of the high peak, the ice, the trickling meltwater. Tiny, quiet, surely seldom seen, she would be a minor power measured against the Snow Chanter or Siddél, but a power she remained, as old as the Wild.

He bowed to her. "Greetings, Blessed One." She didn't answer, and when he looked again, she had become the cat once more.

Marshal's stern voice descended on him. "Bennek, Pantheren has gone back for a rope."

"Good," Bennek called. "We'll need it to climb out again. Now you must jump down, for the Snow Chanter has sent us an emissary."

"What do you mean?"

"There is an Inyomere here, and she has come to show us the way. Do ask Lanyon if she can conjure a light."

They widened the hole in the roof of the fissure. Then Marshal lowered Lanyon, holding her by her wrists. At full reach, her feet swung just above Bennek's head.

"Fall softly," Marshal ordered. "*Now.*"

Lanyon dropped. Bennek caught her, steadying her landing. "You're trembling."

"It's so very cold here."

He started to slip off his coat to put it around her, but she refused. "I have Pantheren's gloves, and you must keep your own warmth. Let us go quickly, and find an end to this."

Next Marshal handed Kit down. Then Pantheren returned with the rope and Marshal used it to descend. Pantheren would wait at the edge of the fissure, ready to help them climb out again.

"We can't survive the night here," he warned them. "If you

haven't found her in half an hour, give it up, and we'll return tomorrow."

"We'll be back within the hour," Marshal promised, "*with* the Snow Chanter."

The leopard had waited patiently during their preparations, but now it set off at a fast pace through the twisting fissure. Bennek raced after it. Kit kept close behind him, but Lanyon, hampered by the rough ice and the hem of her robe, quickly fell behind. Marshal stayed with her, though he couldn't quite hide his impatience.

"I'm sorry," she whispered. "You should go on."

"No. It's I who apologize, and for my brother and cousin too. I won't neglect you, Lanyon. And if it's any consolation, I think they will need you soon enough."

He spoke truly, for as the fissure twisted left and right it descended deeper into the ice, becoming a tunnel with a solid ceiling that allowed no light through. Kit and Bennek soon turned back to meet them.

"I think the Inyomere has gone on," Kit reported. "But it's become so dark, we can't see to take another step. Lanyon, can you make a light?"

"I can. That is a simple spell. Give me your hand."

She slipped off a glove, and told Kit to do the same. Then she took his bare hand in hers, and while his skin was cold, hers was like the ice.

"Cup your hand," she instructed.

She set her palm over his and whispered a simple chant. A pale glow seeped between her trembling fingers. She took her hand away, revealing an orb of soft white light nestled in Kit's palm. It glowed without heat.

"Turn your hand over," she said.

He obeyed. The light did not fall away, but remained against his palm.

Lanyon put her glove back on, and on they went, with Bennek in the lead, relying on the gleam of Kit's light to find the way. This time Bennek was forced to go slower than he liked, for Kit set a pace Lanyon could manage.

The tunnel was high and narrow, the facets of its fractured walls reflecting Kit's light a thousand times over. All could feel as much as hear a deep bass grinding: the complaint of the ice as it flowed slowly, slowly down the mountain.

They had not gone far when they discovered the snow leopard again. It stood in the tunnel, its tail twitching. Bennek approached it, but this time the leopard growled softly and did not move back.

"We are not to go on," Marshal said.

Kit looked about, perplexed. "There is nothing here."

Bennek went to his knees before the Inyomere. "Blessed Spirit of the Ice, we beg you to guide us to Tayeraisa the Snow Chanter."

The leopard reared back, hissing and spitting.

Bennek shied from its teeth. "Can it be a haunt of Siddél? Sent to trap us?"

"No," Marshal said. "The Snow Chanter *is* here. We have only to discover her."

Lanyon turned to Kit. "There are so many reflections here. Hide the light within your coat."

He did it. Darkness rushed in to fill the tunnel—a breath-stealing darkness tasting of eternal cold.

"I see nothing," Bennek said.

Marshal told him, "Look up."

In the glassy ceiling they could just make out a faint white glow arising from deep within the ice. As their eyes adjusted, the glow gained definition, taking on the shape of a wizened woman with long white hair.

"Tayeraisa," Kit whispered. "She has used Lanyon's simple spell of pale light."

They had found the Snow Chanter, but they could not reach her, for she lay entombed behind many feet of solid ice.

# 11

Marshal drew his sword. "Stand back," he commanded.

They retreated. Bennek looked for the snow leopard, but she had disappeared.

Marshal swung his sword, striking the ice hard, twisting the blade as it hit. A few chips fell away. He struck again, but the ice was as hard as time and the Snow Chanter lay deep. Days would be required to chip her free.

Bennek turned to Lanyon. "You have the fire spell."

"There is nothing here to burn!"

"Do you have some other spell?" Marshal asked. "Something to shatter the ice?"

"No! I don't know any—" Her hand went to her mouth.

"What is it?" Bennek asked. "What are you thinking?"

"The arrow." She took off the strap that held Édan's arrow against her back. Kneeling in the bitter cold, she unwrapped the bundle. All watched with great curiosity. They were surprised to see that the bundle contained not just the arrow, but also a carved stick of strange design, with a small hook at one end and a grip at the other.

The arrow itself was beautiful. Its shaft was silver, worked with a spiral of gold, and its feathers were white. Prayers were inscribed all over its mirrored arrowhead. The carved stick looked dull beside it, but Lanyon stripped off her gloves and picked up the stick first.

"What is that?" Bennek asked her.

"Have you not seen such before? It's a spear-thrower. I did not have time or skill to make a bow, but this I could manage. We played games with these when I was a child, though I made this one to fit the nock of the arrow."

"But how is it used?"

She picked up the arrow and stood. "Stand away and I will show you."

Her bare fingers ached with cold; she could not stop their trembling. Still, she managed to fit the nock of the arrow against the spear-thrower's hook. The fingers of her right hand curled around the grip, balancing the arrow's shaft. She cocked her arm.

Since the arrow was a physical object, anyone might cast it. But the spell it carried was fickle and shifting, like a weight sliding on the shaft. It would unbalance the arrow's flight and send it spinning wild unless she imposed her will and guided it through the Mere.

Fixing her mind on the spell's path, she drew a soft breath—and then she hurled the arrow. It struck the ice with tremendous force. White cracks shot through the tunnel walls. Deathly cold flooded the Mere. The cold shot back along the arrow's path. It entered Lanyon's fingertips. She screamed in pain and dropped the spear-thrower, scuttling back as massive blocks of ice crashed to the floor.

Kit dove in to scoop up the spear-thrower and the winding cloth a moment before the ice buried them. The light he carried filled the tunnel and danced in a thousand sliding facets.

When the last shrill notes of falling ice finally died away Kit said, "She has a stronger arm than you, Marshal."

Above them, where the wall and ceiling had fallen, the right hand of the Snow Chanter lay exposed—the nails white as frost and the skin shriveled, wrinkled, clinging tightly around her delicate finger bones. The rest of her body remained entombed.

Lanyon closed her eyes, desperate to leave that place. The cold of the ice possessed her. Her bones ached with it, her chest hurt with every breath, and her heart beat slower and slower as it descended into its own timeless winter. "Help me find the arrow," she begged. "Please."

Bennek leaped onto the pile of fallen ice, kicking and shoving the blocks aside until he uncovered the arrow. He brought it to Lanyon, and again she balanced it with the spear-thrower, and cocked her arm.

"Lanyon," Marshal said with quiet urgency. He pointed to the ceiling, where an ominous net of white cracks had infiltrated the clear ice. "Perhaps you should strike more gently this time."

Lanyon nodded, and launched the arrow again.

Again, the ice shattered, but this time it collapsed in a hailstorm of glittering pebbles that clattered with the voices of a thousand tiny knives all dropped at once. Lanyon fell to her knees, undone by a second wave of cold lashing through her in the backwash of the spell.

Still, the spell had worked. Tayeraisa was free.

The Snow Chanter lay limp, half-buried in the avalanche of crumbled ice. She was nude and skeletally thin, her white skin shrunken and stretched over bones that could be counted even in Kit's pale light. Her hair was a tangled white mat. Her breasts, empty sacs. Anyone would have taken her for a corpse, except she blinked. The eyes that looked on them from that faded being gleamed blue as the bluest sky.

Marshal clambered to her across the loose ice. He scooped her up, finding her as light as a child in his arms. He carried her beyond the debris, and then laid her down again. Slipping off his own coat, he dressed her in it. "Blessed One," he whispered, "you called us and we have come."

Her chest rose as she drew a deep breath, a breath of satisfaction, so it seemed. Marshal helped her to sit up. She smiled at him, and her gaze lingered on his face for many seconds. Then she turned to look at Bennek and then at Kit. "My sons," she whispered, as a rosy flush touched her cheeks. "I live again because you heeded my call."

Both fell to their knees.

"You are our ancestor," Marshal said. "The mother of our people. You have our love and our loyalty, Blessed One. You honor us by your return."

She closed her eyes and breathed deeply again. "Do you know what a dangerous thing you've done by freeing me?"

"Ma'am?"

She looked at Marshal again, and her gaze grew hard. "I know the lies Siddél has spread. He has led my own people to believe I destroyed myself. Is this not so?"

Marshal was taken aback. He looked to Kit, but found no help there. He turned to Lanyon.

She too knelt on the ice. The cold had driven all color from her face so that even her lips were pale, and she was shivering so hard she had not gotten her gloves back on. Even so, she spoke boldly when she answered the Snow Chanter. "It *is* so, Blessed One. It's said you were overcome with grief after the passing of Samoket, and gave yourself up to the Mere."

"That is a lie of Siddél. It was not grief that drove me to the ice. It was Siddél himself. My enemy. That great thundering monster!"

Lanyon nodded. "I have a thing to show you, Far Mother."

Bennek guessed what she intended. He went back into the broken ice. Again he found the arrow and brought it to her.

Tayeraisa craned her withered neck to see. "What is that evil thing?"

"It is a talisman bound to the Mere with a spell that will slay Siddél."

"You cannot slay Siddél. He is no petty Inyomere. The Snow Leopard you might destroy, and never again would the call of those cats be heard amid the peaks; or if you murdered the fish-silver spirit of a stream, then ever after its waters would be foul. But Siddél is the thunder and the storm, and such a power may never be extinguished from the world."

Lanyon heard these words and despair came over her, but to the Snow Chanter she said, "Then you speak my doom, for nevertheless, I will try."

This resolve pleased Tayeraisa, and she smiled. "It is not possible for you to slay Siddél," she repeated. "Still, it may be that you could use this evil weapon to destroy his form, separate him from his flesh, sever his awareness so that he cannot practice his magic or his malice. Such was the fate he wished on me."

Hope returned to Lanyon and she smiled despite the crushing cold. "I think that would be enough," she conceded in a rasping voice.

Tayeraisa chuckled.

Marshal found it confounding, as if a corpse lay laughing in his arms. "We should go," he said nervously. "We have overstayed our time and Pantheren will be desperate. Kit, go first and light the way. Bennek, see to Lanyon. All haste now!"

He reached to lift Tayeraisa again, but to their surprise she stood up on her own.

"I am not my old self," she told them, swaying on her feet. "Not yet, though that will change, thanks to the devotion of my children." She turned a discerning gaze on Lanyon. "I know all my children, no matter how changed. You, I will name my little sister."

Lanyon bowed again, honored at this compliment, though troubled, too. She wondered what change the Snow Chanter sensed.

Bennek came to her, and with his help she re-wrapped Édan's arrow and the spear-thrower in their winding cloth. "I am so cold," she whispered to him. "I can't bear to feel the arrow against me."

"Let me carry it for you."

He took the bundle and looped it over his back. Then he slipped an arm around her waist to steady her, while the Snow Chanter accepted Marshal's offer of support.

They made their way back through the tunnel and into the fissure, to find that full night had descended, bringing with it a fierce cold, much worse than in the deep reaches of the ice tunnel.

Marshal whistled, and Pantheren answered him at once, "What report?"

"We are safe, and we have found her."

They made their way off the ice, guided by starlight. Kina paid them an ecstatic greeting.

The cold had become an iron presence. All sounds of water

dripping and trickling had ceased. Lanyon could not stop shaking, nor feel her fingers or toes.

In haste they retreated into the pass, taking shelter at last in a copse of ancient, twisted evergreens. Kit's light had faded and Lanyon was too weary to create another, so they groped for dead wood in the dark. Then Lanyon called the name of the fire spell, setting the pile instantly ablaze.

The alpine night turned their breath to frost and transformed the water skins to solid ice, but Tayeraisa the Snow Chanter thrived despite the cold. She sat cross-legged before the fire with Marshal's coat draped loosely about her, staring trance-like into the flames.

She had retreated into herself and would not speak. Nor would she accept any food or water. Instead she seemed to nourish herself from the frigid air and the fire's dancing light. Hour by hour, her appearance changed. Life filled her shriveled skin. A flush of gold crept through the tangled white mass of her hair. Flesh gathered in the hollows of her cheeks, and a white mist draped her body like a garment weaving itself into existence.

Lanyon sat across from her, huddled close to the fire, and no longer was it possible to mistake her for one of the Inyomere. Her frailty was all too clear as she hugged herself and shivered within her robe.

Bennek crouched beside her. "Are you not warmer now?"

"No," she whispered past the chattering of her teeth. "When I used Édan's arrow, the cold of the ice passed into me. I cannot stop shaking. I can hardly feel the warmth of the fire. If I were to climb into it I think it would not hurt me."

"Lanyon! You must not say such things. I'll help you to get warm. Here, I've brought you my blanket. I'll put it around you."

"It won't help. There is no heat inside me."

"I'll warm the blanket by the flames."

"No. Just sit with me. Put the blanket around both of us. Let me share your warmth."

He frowned awkwardly, but he did as she asked, and in a few

minutes her shivering subsided and a ruddy flush touched her cheeks. "You're warmer now?" he asked.

She nodded. "But please stay with me a while more." She leaned her head against his shoulder and stared past the flames at Tayeraisa, lost in her Inyomere trance. Her chest rose and fell with long, slow breaths, and firelight danced in her glassy eyes.

"Watch her," Lanyon said softly. "She draws the heat inside herself, and with every passing moment she grows stronger."

"You freed her," Bennek said. "That's where your strength has gone. You should sleep now. Rest. You look so tired."

"Will you lie down with me? I'm afraid of the cold. If I could lie between you and the fire, I think I will be all right."

Again Bennek felt awkward; he didn't know what to say.

"I'm sorry," Lanyon whispered.

"No! Of course I'll do all I can for you. My turn at the watch comes late. So let's lie here by the fire and you'll become warm. I am warm now."

"I know it. You're warmer than the fire."

They lay down together beneath the blanket. Bennek felt her hair against his face and the curve of her body against his belly. He gazed at her cheek and the line of her shoulder. He knew he was breathing too fast. Other things moved in him too. "It's so hot now," he whispered. "I think we are too close to the fire."

"No, it is perfect." Her words slurred, as if she spoke from the edge of sleep. "You have saved my life, Bennek."

"Will you teach me the fire spell, then?"

"I have told you that I would. Not tonight though. I am so tired."

"Tomorrow, then. Lanyon, are you not hot?"

"I'm just right . . . but what of the arrow? Is it safe?"

"It's with my pack."

She nodded, and slowly her breathing steadied until he knew she was asleep. He didn't think he would ever sleep, but it wasn't much later that his eyes closed too.

# 12

Bennek woke abruptly, overcome by alarm, certain something had gone amiss. Lanyon still lay beside him. The fire still burned with ruddy coals. But beyond the sheltering boughs of the stunted evergreens, dawn's first light already gleamed in the sky—and he had not yet served his turn at the watch.

He rolled out from under the blanket and sat up, looking for his bow and some evidence of disaster. But both Kit and Pantheren slept quietly by the fire, while at the edge of the grove Marshal kept the watch, his tall figure silhouetted against the pale sky. Kina sat beside him, her sharp gaze following something in the pass beyond.

Bennek found his bow, and silently, he ran to join Marshal. As he reached the edge of the trees the pass spread out before him. He was startled to see a pale figure walking there. At first he took it for a ghost.

"That is Tayeraisa," Marshal said softly. "She has been walking under starlight for many hours. Her beauty has returned, and the wind has combed her hair into long tresses of pale gold."

"You haven't slept?" Bennek asked. "You've watched all night?"

"No. Pantheren and Kit have shared the watch."

"Why did Kit not wake me? It was my turn after his."

Marshal gave his brother a cool look. "I told him I would take your turn. Lanyon had need of you. It wounded her to use Édan's arrow. It let the ice take her warmth."

"It's true she couldn't escape the cold. The fire would not warm her."

"Pantheren said that sometimes it's only the warmth of life that can reach a chilled soul . . . but it would not do for me or Kit or Pantheren to lie with her, for we are men. You're only a boy. That's why she could ask you to keep her warm."

This stung, for Bennek could not recall any failure of deed that would lead Marshal to say such a thing. "I am as much a man as you, Marshal!"

"You are fifteen," Marshal said. "A full two years younger than Kit and I."

"A man is measured by his deeds, not his years."

"In the hunt that is true, but women have other measures."

"You want to shame me!"

"I do not! I tell you these things so you will not feel any shame over this night. There has been no disrespect because you are still a boy."

"Is it disrespectful then, to lie with a woman? I know there was a woman in Habaddon whom you would visit, Marshal. Did you keep her warm while her husband was cold in the grave?"

"That is something you are too young to understand." He raised his hand to stop Bennek from speaking. "Say no more. Your ill temper leads you to unseemly speech, when silence would serve you better. Go now to scout the cliff's edge. I would know if there are arowl in the lands below. Go, and leave your wrath to wither in the fields."

Lanyon awakened in time to witness some of this exchange. She could not make out their words, but the tenor was clear. Some of the chill of the night returned to her. It didn't help when she turned to find Pantheren awake and watching her with somber eyes.

"Are you well, Lanyon Kyramanthes?"

"As well as may be."

Bennek had gone, but he had left Édan's arrow beside his pack, so she retrieved it. The bundle felt cold in her hands, but it was not the monstrous cold of the ice flow, so she took it again into her care.

Kit awoke, and soon Marshal returned to the encampment with Tayeraisa. Her transformation was startling to see. During the night her skin had become smooth and flush, her hair full and touched with the palest shade of gold. She had conjured herself a long tunic and soft pants of a dusky golden hue t0 match the high valley's autumn heath. She laughed easily, and her eyes sparkled with the joy of new-found freedom.

Pantheren met her and bowed, for there had been no chance for him to pay his respects before, in their desperate haste to leave the ice field.

The Snow Chanter regarded him, saying, "You are not Samokeän, but belong to Jahallon's people, I think."

"You read it right, ma'am, though Habaddon has been home to Samokea-in-exile these many years." He sighed. "It is a wonder to me that you're here. There is so much I would ask you, so much I would know, but there is no time. The season is late, and I fear that if we do not flee these heights, Siddél will bring a storm to waylay us."

"I share this fear. I will dream of his dissolution, but I am drained of strength, and must shelter and recuperate. If I meet Siddél as I am now, I will fall to him again."

"Then let us breakfast swiftly," Marshal said, "and move on in haste, though I don't know what shelter we can hope to find."

"These mountains are my dominion," Tayeraisa reminded him. "I have many hidden places where we may take shelter. The closest is only a few hours to the north, in the low hills that face the eastern prairie."

So they ate a hasty breakfast and set out, even before Bennek returned. He met them near the eastern end of the pass, reporting that the lands below appeared abandoned, with nothing moving larger than a bird.

To the relief of all, the Snow Chanter did not ask them to climb down the cliff wall. Instead, she led them on an easy track north through the mountains.

As the morning aged, gray clouds gathered around the peaks and a light snow began to fall. It frosted the ground but did not hinder them as they descended, first through low groves of gnarled and twisted evergreens, and then stands of tall cedar and hemlock. The evergreen forest eventually gave way to broad-leaved trees ablaze with their autumn finery, and still the snow fell, following them down and down into the foothills. The Snow Chanter delighted in it, joyous as the soft flakes swirled around her.

In early afternoon they came on a stream that ran chattering through the forest, and this they followed to the forest's edge. Here the trees stood guard as the plain rolled up against the feet of the Tiyat-kel. They gazed out over the sweep of the grassland, but the air was misty and they could not see far.

"We are come to the eastern edge of my home," Tayeraisa said. "Long ago, I named this place Medesh. I have not been here in oh so many seasons. Not since I met Samoket, for I never crossed to the eastern side of the mountains when I knew him." Then she laughed at their confusion, for she had promised them shelter, but they saw only the prairie, the trees, the mountains. "Come!" she said merrily. "You must endure only a few more steps to find the comfort promised you."

She turned toward the stream, and now they saw a graceful bridge arching over it, and on the other side a beautiful white house appeared. It had rafters of polished red wood that ended in upward sweeping curves, and a roof of golden thatch. The wide front door looked to be made of beaten gold. A porch ran all around, and from the chimney a curl of gray smoke wound up into the sky.

"Who is at home?" Marshal wondered, as he reached up for the hilt of his sword.

"We are!" the Snow Chanter answered with a laugh. "I do not know what passes in this house when I am away, but if ever I return, it's as if I have only just left."

"As if the house has stepped through time," Lanyon whispered, but the Snow Chanter had already hurried across the bridge and did not hear her.

The cottage door opened onto a large room. The Snow Chanter

circled it, throwing open shutters, filling the house with the day's glimmering light. In the fireplace, neatly stacked embers burned hot beneath jackets of gray ash. Soft white rugs lay scattered across the stone tiles of the floor. At the center of the room, cushions surrounded a low, polished table that held a bowl of fresh, fragrant camellias. And on a sideboard, a brush and inkpot kept company with a lacquered box holding squares of white paper for the writing of prayers to be released within the fire.

Kina stood at the door and whined, but Pantheren commanded her to stay outside.

"You will be hungry," Tayeraisa said as she opened cabinets. "I don't partake much of food, but there are things here that Samoket enjoyed."

Kit went to look. "There is bread!" he announced. "Dried meat, cheese, dried fruits, and milk. How can there be milk? There is not a cow."

"Maybe it's goat's milk?" Pantheren suggested with a grin.

"Is any of it real?" Bennek wondered, picking up a small loaf and sniffing at it suspiciously. He bit into it. Evidently it was real enough, for he finished it quickly.

"There is a bathhouse," Tayeraisa remembered, opening a back door and pointing down a cobbled path that led to a small outbuilding. Smoke puffed from the chimney. They went to look, and discovered a hearty fire heating a round brass tub filled with water piped from the stream. An overflow of warm water fed a shower a few steps below the level of the tub.

None of them had ever seen anything so wonderful. Not even Pantheren, who had lived in the great southern city of Hallah for a year.

Lanyon went first to bathe. Then, while the men took their turn, she set to preparing a bountiful meal from the stores in Tayeraisa's cabinets. She had just set the food out on the table when Bennek and Pantheren came in.

"Where is the Snow Chanter?" Pantheren wondered. "I would speak with her."

"I am here," Tayeraisa answered, appearing at the front door. "I have brought a gift for Lanyon." Neatly folded over her arm were garments the color of autumn fields. "I made these for you. The black garments you wear now are so like the funeral raiment of a fallen warrior, it saddens my heart."

Lanyon's cheeks grew warm. "I beg your forgiveness, ma'am. I will discard these somber clothes at once."

"Why do you blush?" Bennek wondered.

"Indeed," Pantheren said. "Now you have stirred our curiosity. Where did you come by these garments?"

Lanyon looked scandalized. "I will not say."

She took the clothing Tayeraisa had given her and returned a few minutes later, dressed in soft brown pants and tunic, and calf-high leather boots. Édan's arrow now rested in a sturdy leather case fitted with a fur-padded strap. There was also a long coat of tight weave and great warmth, but this Lanyon set aside, for it was pleasant within the house.

Pantheren looked her over with an amused gaze, but Bennek eyed her with dark suspicion. "Your old garments *were* funeral raiment, weren't they?" he accused. "That's why you will not say."

"They are gone now."

"Why did you dress so? Do you have a death wish, Lanyon? Did you await your own last rites?"

She turned to him, outraged. "It was not like that!"

"Then what?" he insisted.

"Bennek, they were only clothes!"

"Whose clothes?" Pantheren wondered.

Lanyon made a cry of exasperation. "Has the Snow Chanter not already told you? They are the raiment of the dead. I took them from a tomb that I passed on the road from the Citadel. Bennek! Do not make such an expression of distaste. The garments were not foul. There was a magic protecting that grave, and the fallen warrior who wore them was not corrupt."

"But . . . you despoiled a grave," Bennek muttered, as if this was an impossible thought.

"By necessity! The night was freezing."

"Sacredness must bow to necessity," Pantheren said, his eyes crinkling with silent laughter.

"How did the warrior look?" Tayeraisa wondered. "For all but the Inyomere must finally pass from the world."

"He was passing," Lanyon agreed. "His flesh was ethereal— whole and smooth but possessing a lightness as if the substance of him was gradually leaving. I expect that some day he will vanish without ever being touched by decay."

"Very pretty," Pantheren said. "The Samokeäns have always been the cleverest of the people. But Bennek, you do not look well."

"I am fine!"

The Snow Chanter frowned at him. "Pantheren is right. You should lie down and rest."

"Do not fear the houses of the dead!" Pantheren advised him. "They are the houses of our ancestors, who can only wish us well. Even those neglected ghosts whose graves lie unmarked beneath the open sky do not bear us ill will."

# 13

They slept through the afternoon, so in the evening they were wakeful and full of questions for the Snow Chanter. How had she come to be in the ice? When had Siddél become her enemy? Why did the Inyomere of the Wild despise the people? Why had she loved Samoket?

She smiled. "Your questions are many! And still there are things you have not asked and do not understand. If you will, I will tell you a brief tale of the Wild. Some parts of this story you know, but others will be new to you, and when I am done you'll have the answers to your questions, and to many you have not asked."

Pantheren took out his red prayer banner so that he might work on it as she spoke. Bennek took out a precious needle and thread to repair a small tear in his coat. Then they gathered together around the slow-burning fire and the Snow Chanter began her tale.

"Long ago, I invited the raging thunderstorm into these mountains. We were akin, Siddél and I. I was the snow and winter's cold. He was the storm. We would meet and play in the mountains, both of us fascinated by the austerity of the heights and the endless dance of clouds—while knowing little of the living things of forest, prairie, and ocean. I think now this put us at a distance from our own kind, and led us to a fascination with the people, for you were like us in the way you were drawn to the spirits of rock and metal and mountain.

"But in that time when the people first came to the shores of the Wild, all the Inyomere looked on you in dread. The unending building, the discipline of the farms, the uncountable babies born in any season, the endless hunting, and of the best stock, not the poorest! You seemed to us to be a plague that could consume all the Wild.

"So we drew together in counsel—the first time such a thing was ever done. Some among us were resolved that the people should be destroyed so the Wild could continue as it always had been, and Siddél was first among these. Some few of us protested that there must be a purpose to your existence. But most of the Inyomere abandoned the counsel saying, 'Let fate fall as it may,' for that has always been our way.

"It is easy to say, 'I will not do this thing.' But among the Inyomere it is hardly possible to say, 'You will not do this thing.' Those who heeded Siddél looked at the people and declared them weak, for you did not have fangs, claws, horns, or the will of the Inyomere. You were prey. So it seemed an act of perfect balance that they should make a hunter, one that was ruthless and endowed with an instinct to consume only the people, and when the last person was gone from the Wild, the hunter would die away and all would be as it was.

"Vanity!

"The Inyomere did not make the Wild, or any of the life that inhabits it. Long ago, One came and wakened us, and the Wild was as it was, whole and beautiful. We lived within the uncounted seasons, nurturing the life of the valleys and mountains, the glades and the prairies, the streams and the lakes and the shore. But none of that life was made by us. It had its existence just as we had ours, from the will of Another.

"Siddél would not accept this. 'It is only that we have been content,' he argued, 'so that we were not moved to create something new and beautiful.' He was wrong. What he finally made was not life. The arowl are abominations. Monsters twisted from the essence of natural creatures. They cannot make more of their own kind, but must always be made anew from the malice of Siddél.

"It was not long before even Siddél's allies rued what had been done, for the arowl were maddened by their own abomination and their instinct was corrupt. In the absence of the people they fell upon the natural creatures of the Wild, killing even when they were not hungry. There is an agony in their nature eased only by the taste of blood. But Siddél was not abased by this horror. He set it aside and urged his pets south. The fate of the people seemed fixed . . . save that a vision came to Jahallon.

"I do not know what Inyomere sent him this warning, or if it was a gift from the One who wakened us all, but if not for Jahallon's foresight the people might well have been overrun before they knew their peril.

"But even as the first arowl were being forced into existence, Jahallon suffered a nightmare like none known to the people before. In his dream he watched horrid beasts assailing his friends, slaying them with teeth and claws. He called these beasts arowl after the great clamor they made as they attacked. The same nightmare came to him again and again, and all who knew of it called it a corrupt vision and warned him to put it from his mind, but he would not.

"It seemed to those who loved him that he was driven mad. Instead of building a homestead, he made a smithy, and instead of wooing a wife, he practiced at smelting long knives that he called swords, and great spears more brutal than the fishing spears the people had known. He persuaded the young men to spar with these things. Their elders did not approve, but the youth called it a sport and it was allowed. Jahallon also made a vast stock of great bows, and arrows so heavy they were of no use in hunting. His father grieved, believing he had lost his son to these evil dreams.

"Then in the third year after the people came to the Wild, the arowl packs reached the settled lands. The outlying farms were overrun and utterly destroyed—save where Jahallon's companions had made their homes. In such places, the people's swords and great bows brought terror to the arowl, which passed them by.

"In those days the city of Hallah had no fortifications. Many of the people were taken by surprise and slaughtered, but others remembered Jahallon's vision, and when the arowl came, they rushed to grab staffs and pitchforks and hunting bows. Jahallon himself rallied his companions, and brought slaughter on the beasts that had been sent to slaughter them, and the people ever after have counted that day a victory, though many hundreds were lost.

"That was the beginning of the Long War. Many years would pass before the arowl came again and in that time the people came to believe their first victory was final—but peace is not in the nature of Siddél, or of Jahallon.

"I am bound to these mountains and do not wander, but Siddél is not so constrained. He was moved by the bravery of the people and the cleverness of Jahallon, and regretted making the arowl. So he went to Hallah to seek Jahallon, and he found him in his smithy.

"Siddél was entranced by the making of things within the heat of the forge, but Jahallon was wary, for the Inyomere of the Wild were not like the Inyomere he had known in his youth in Hahví, and he mistrusted Siddél.

"Siddél did not perceive this, for he had no understanding of the people. When Jahallon asked him how such abominable creatures as the arowl had come into the Wild, it did not occur to Siddél to dissemble or evade. He answered Jahallon truthfully, for the Inyomere do not lie.

"So Jahallon heard from the monster himself the tale of the arowl, and rage possessed him. He seized his spear and sought to slay him, but Siddél is the storm. He drew that raiment about himself and fled with his wound.

"To Siddél, Jahallon's rash act proved that the people were wanton and violent. All his hatred was renewed. He resolved to hunt the people until none remained in the Wild—but for Jahallon he reserved a special fate, pronounced that night in a curse Jahallon heard in his dreams, and the curse was that Jahallon would be endowed somewhat with the will of the Inyomere, so that he would be safe from death, though not from pain, and for that Jahallon has paid in grief and suffering far beyond the measure of any man.

"The Long War was renewed. The arowl came again, though this time they came armed with swords, spears, and bows, like the people. Terrible battles were fought, and the course of the war was ever unpredictable. Sometimes the arowl would not be seen for years and men would ride north and seek them, killing any they found. At other times the arowl would rise again in great packs and descend on the people.

"Hallah was fortified, and the other settlements as well. Then Jahallon led his people into the north. After Habaddon was founded, the battles grew fiercer, and there were not men enough to push deeper into the Wild. I dwell in the southern Tiyat-kel, which begins just a little north of the Glycian River, and still it was many years before any of the people dared to cross.

"But Samoket came to me at last. I sensed him as a stir, a flurry in the Expanse. His was a fiery soul. He had come north in defiance of his father, Jahallon. He came seeking metal ores, and he was alone. The arowl failed to slay him only because he had a talent to beguile their minds and send them fleeing in fear. He was the first of the people I ever beheld and he was beautiful—as all his people after him are beautiful—and he could touch my mind as if he were Inyomere, though he was not.

"Never before had I known anything like him. I was fascinated, and could not turn away. I changed myself to become what he desired, for carnality is not a trait of the Inyomere. Later, I changed myself further to bear him children. Forty-two beautiful babies I brought into the world! And oh! Siddél was madly jealous. For with my children I created life that was beautiful, balanced and true, while everything Siddél had ever made was malformed and wicked.

"Would that those years in the Citadel had gone on forever! It is the way of the Inyomere that the Wild continues on as it was, and is, and always will be. But it is the way of the people that all things change.

"The day came when Samoket abandoned me, crossing over to that place only the ghosts of the people have seen. I was confounded and so I retired to the high peaks, to think on all that I had learned of the people.

"Siddél found me there, when I was deep in thought and aware of naught but the soft falling of the snow. In his fearful imaginings, he had come to believe that I had lain with Samoket only to glean from him the people's power to create life, and he was sure I would use this knowledge against him.

"So he sought to destroy me. I am no petty Inyomere, and I may not be extinguished from the world. Still, he stunned me with his lightning and with his great sword he defiled my body so that I was broken. My blood drained away and I could not warm myself or resist him, but I refused to abandon my existence. So he took me and imprisoned me deep within the ice.

"He had tried to separate me from my flesh, and he had very nearly succeeded. My will still drove the snows, for the Inyomere are only the waking face of all aspects of the Wild. I am the snow and the cold of winter, and that will go on even if my awareness should fail. Awareness is a gift of the One, and it may be taken away, or returned at will to the Expanse.

"For many years I barely held on. I knew only a flickering existence until the snow leopard sensed me in the ice. She is an Inyomere without speech or name, but she has always been devoted to me. Though she could not rescue me from the ice, she led me back to myself. As I recovered my strength, I called for help from the rain, the wind, the birds that flew above the peaks in the summer, but none dared incur Siddél's wrath, so they pretended not to hear. But Siddél knew I was awake.

"I am aware of much that has passed since my fall, because Siddél himself brought me the news. His thunder has raged over these peaks time and again, bringing me gloating word of his misdeeds in the Wild. So I know the Citadel is fallen, and that many of my children are slain ... but not all.

"Now, finally, the children of Tayeraisa and Samoket have returned to the north, and by their valor, I live again in the Wild."

*Medesh*

# 14

EARLY THE NEXT morning, Pantheren startled awake at the snap of a bow. Dim light pervaded the cottage, allowing him to make out at least two figures still asleep on the floor. He arose in silence, his own bow and a quiver of arrows in hand.

He had slept close to the cottage door. Now he opened it cautiously and peered outside, to see the eastern horizon aglow with a blue light that chased the stars away and glistened against little caps of snow dusting each plume of tall grass. He heard whispering voices and soft laughter, then the sound of the bow again, followed by the sharp *whack* of an arrow as it found a target of wood.

Stepping around the corner of the porch, he discovered Lanyon with a bow in hand, and beside her Bennek, giving advice, and despite the dim light, Pantheren could not miss the admiration in her eyes.

Last night they had all sat in rapt silence until the Snow Chanter finished her tale, but afterward Marshal and Kit had made much of Bennek's talent for confounding the arowl.

"Blessed One, he is like Samoket in this," Marshal had said. "He has this gift from our far father, that he may beguile and terrify the beasts."

Kit had been as proud. "If my cousin had not been blessed with Samoket's gift, we would not have won past the arowl. We would not have been able to come to you."

But Bennek was not Samoket. He was not Édan. He was a boy, and it was foolish for Lanyon to see him as something more.

Kina lay in the shadows. She thumped her tail when she saw Pantheren—and Bennek turned to look. He flinched in surprise when he saw Pantheren standing there, and Lanyon was so confounded she recoiled.

Pantheren spoke in a stern voice. "Bennek, it is your turn at watch. Did you not hear me stir?"

"War Father, I confess I did not."

"I was brought awake by the sound of the bow. Was it only a game?"

"No, sir. It seemed wise that Lanyon should try her bow and learn the feel of it before we set out."

"Her bow?"

Lanyon recovered herself, bringing the weapon for him to see. "War Father, please don't be angry. The bow was beside me when I woke. The Snow Chanter must have left it. Feel how light it is! It's easy for me to draw."

Pantheren felt the weight of it, and ran his hands along its length. In the low light he could just make out the glint of prayers written in the wood. He handed it back to her.

"You're not pleased with it?" she asked.

"This should have been Édan's task, not yours. But we do what we can."

The day began in warmth, with the snow melting quickly once the sun rose, but the season was late, and Pantheren worried that before long the weather would turn against them. "We must go on quickly. Our best hope—maybe our only hope—is to find the Storm Lair before winter sets in."

They all agreed, but when they looked for the Snow Chanter to tell her their decision, they could not find her. No one had seen her since the evening.

"Perhaps she has returned to the peaks," Lanyon suggested.

The boys refused to believe it. "No doubt she has her own tasks," Kit allowed, "but she'll return again by the time we're ready to depart."

So they prepared their packs, fattening them with food from

the cottage, taking all they could reasonably carry, and before long they were ready to leave. The Snow Chanter, though, still had not returned. Doubt descended on them. Should they wait? Already, gray clouds gathered in the sky, but they were loath to go without wishing the Snow Chanter farewell.

Then Bennek announced what no one wanted to hear. "There's a small pack of ten arowl to the south. They are far away, and I don't think they will find our trail. Still, it may be best if we go on while the arowl are few."

"Bennek is right," Pantheren said. "We must go while we can. The Snow Chanter has affirmed our task and knows our urgency. She will understand that it's necessity, and not discourtesy, that has made us leave."

So they shuttered the house and set out. At first they looked back hoping to see Tayeraisa appear on the porch, but after a few more steps the house faded from sight as if it had never been.

"We will see her again," Marshal said softly, though doubt was in his voice.

North of Medesh, a series of low hills skirted the foot of the higher mountains. Toothy outcroppings of gray rock crowned many of their summits, and between them lay a winding succession of meadows.

Marshal felt safer following those meadows, rather than returning to the open grasslands where they had encountered the stampeding arowl. So they set out that way.

It was a pretty landscape, aglow with autumn colors despite a heavy cloud cover, and all around, birds sang out in celebration. But as they walked, Marshal felt a dark foreboding settle over him. After only half an hour, he called a halt.

"Perhaps it is the absence of the Snow Chanter," he told the others. "But I am uneasy. Bennek, take a few minutes. See what lies around us."

Bennek obeyed, sitting cross-legged before entering his trance. Marshal watched his brother as the minutes passed, disturbed at the deepening concern he saw on his Bennek's youthful face.

At last, Bennek opened his eyes. "We're not alone here," he announced urgently. He looked up at Marshal. "I can scarcely believe it, but south of us are two warriors on horseback, riding fast, with the arowl pack I saw before snapping at their heels. Why they don't turn and fight I cannot say. The beasts that pursue them are few in number, though there are were-beasts and a dire wolf among them."

"They are likely wounded," Pantheren said. "Remember the stampede of arowl we witnessed. These are surely desperate survivors of some battle to the south."

"There is another thing," Bennek said. "I tried to spread fear among the pack but they were distracted for only a moment. I don't know what to make of it."

Kit said, "I think once they taste blood, they're not easily dissuaded."

Marshal felt the strain of divided obligations. Their task was to escort Lanyon north to the Storm Lair, but he could not leave two wounded warriors to fall to the arowl. "We must go to their aid," he decided, and all agreed.

They turned, jogging back the way they had come, and very soon they heard the distant hue and cry of the pack—a bone-chilling clamor that guided them east toward the plain.

Rounding a small hill, they came on a long meadow that went on for half a mile before it spilled into the wide grasslands. They followed the meadow, staying close to the groves and thickets that bounded it on the north.

The arowl were not yet in sight, but as they neared the plain, Marshal saw the riders. And to his surprise—to the surprise of everyone, Bennek most of all—there were three horsemen, not two.

"Take cover," Marshal ordered.

Bennek obeyed, dropping back among the trees, but he argued against what they had all just seen. "Marshal, there were not three!" he insisted. "I swear it. I was among them and there were only two."

"Did you also miscount the arowl?" Kit asked with scorn.

"I don't know," Bennek admitted. "I don't know what happened."

Pantheren sent Lanyon up the hill, to shelter in a ridge of tumbled rocks that spilled down from the low summit.

"Go with her," Marshal told Bennek.

But at this, Bennek bristled. "I mistook the count. That doesn't mean I can't fight."

"Do not dispute with me, Bennek! Do as I say and do it now. Go with Lanyon. Secure yourself. Affect the arowl if you can, but if not, you'll have good vantage to use your bow. Kit and I will stay here among the trees. And Pantheren—"

Marshal turned to look for him, but Pantheren had already slipped away into the thickets, taking Kina with him.

Bennek felt disgruntled, his confidence shaken, as he followed Lanyon up among the rocks. They found a hollow that offered good cover from below while allowing them to look out on the prairie.

"You should get your bow ready," Bennek advised as scattered drops of rain began to fall. "I'll leave my arrows on the ground between us."

Sitting down behind a low wall of sheltering rock, he sought the trance again, determined to understand his mistake. But an anguished cry from Lanyon called him back. "We are too late!"

Bennek turned to see the horsemen racing toward his position, the arowl already among them. Two of the beasts ran like wolves, bounding between the horses as they yammered in bloodcurdling voices. White slashes marked their shoulders just like the dire wolves he'd seen, though these were of ordinary size—150 pounds, no more. Just behind them ran a tall were-beast, white slashes on its face.

Fat drops of rain soaked the rocks as Bennek braced himself against the expected sight of the beasts leaping to attack the warriors—yet seconds passed and it did not happen. Neither did the horsemen mount any defense. Not one of the three had a sword or a spear in hand.

"They are not fleeing," Bennek concluded in astonishment. "They ride *with* the arowl."

Lanyon did not want to believe it. "That's not possible! The arowl cannot be tamed, or taught to forego the people's blood."

But as if to offer further proof, the lead horseman raised his hand, signaling his companions to halt. They pulled up just out of bow range, their horses dancing and shimmying, frantic to distance themselves from the arowl that circled them. The beasts growled and snapped at the horses and at one other, but the riders ignored them.

Their leader wore a dark gray coat, his hood pulled up against the drizzling rain. Gripping the reins of his prancing horse, he turned to speak to his two companions. Neither wore hoods. They were older men with weathered faces, their graying hair in long braids, in the Samokeän style.

Bennek knew there were other arowl somewhere, but he could not see them, not even the dire wolf. "Something is terribly wrong, Lanyon," he whispered, settling down again behind the rock. She looked at him anxiously.

"Keep watch for me?" he asked.

"I will."

As the rain pattered around them, he closed his eyes and turned in the Fourth Way.

At once he saw the two gray-haired riders poised on their trembling horses, luminous in their existence; just as clearly he saw the three circling arowl and the other beasts scattered in the thickets, the dire wolf among them, all of them marked with white slashes; he saw Marshal's bright presence, creeping in stealth through a dense grove, moving ever closer to the horsemen, with Kit following close behind; and he saw Pantheren in the rocks, not far from his own position—but he could not see the hooded rider or the horse he rode.

Bennek retreated from the Mere. In an urgent whisper, he told Lanyon, "The hooded one is a sorcerer. He's hidden within the Mere just as you are, and all the arowl that accompany him are marked with white scars."

"Should we kill him?" she asked, holding her bow with an arrow fitted to the string.

Bennek drew back in shock. "He is of the people!"

"He rides with the arowl. He has marked them as his own. He has betrayed the people!"

Bennek shook his head, unwilling to speak of such things. "I must return to the Mere. The arowl are scattered, and we are vulnerable."

Drizzling rain fell as Marshal gazed past a screen of leaves and branches. The three riders had stopped to talk together out in the meadow, ignoring the trio of arowl that stalked around them.

"Is it real?" Kit whispered.

Marshal nodded. The frantic, prancing, eye-rolling fear of the horses told him it *was* real. This was not some evil vision. These men rode with tame arowl.

He listened, but could not make out what the men said. The two without hoods gazed south, back the way they had come. One got out his spear.

Then a distant chorus of howls drifted in across the still air and Marshal understood their concern. His heart beat faster. Soon there would be many more arowl.

The tall were-beast also noticed the howling of the approaching pack. It drew from its belt the two crude swords it carried, and it bellowed a challenge, baring its yellow fangs to the rain. The two wolfish beasts offered up their own howls—cries echoed at once by pack mates that Marshal hadn't seen yet, hidden in the thickets.

The horses could not endure it. Two reared, the third bucked against the restraint of its bridle, and amid this chaos whatever spell of restraint had held the arowl in check abruptly failed.

The two wolfish arowl leaped together toward the hooded rider. A shouted warning from one of the gray-hairs—"*Aidin!*"—and a spear impaled one of the attacking arowl in the ribs. Marshal launched his own arrow, piercing the second wolfish beast in the spinal cord. As the two arowl fell to the ground, the hooded rider—Aidin?—turned with a knife in his hand, and cast it at the were-beast, piercing its throat as it tried to leap on one of his companion's horses.

At this affront, the arowl hiding in the thickets threw off all restraint. The dire wolf plunged into the open, charging the horsemen while uttering a bloodcurdling howl. Two smaller beasts closed on Marshal's position. The others picked up the intoxicating scent of prey from among the rocks and went leaping after it.

Bennek sat entranced, his spirit-self at large within the Mere, when chaos erupted among the arowl. Their blood-hunger had been held off by the will of the sorcerer, but no longer. They were maddened, and all restraint was gone.

He set loose a miasma of fear among the two arowl closest to Marshal and Kit, but his efforts did nothing to slow their attack. Marshal met the first with his sword, but even as he sliced open its throat the other leaped on him, knocking him to the ground.

Bennek's spirit-self followed the beast down. He descended so swiftly that he fell into its mind. Its seething rage engulfed him; he was immersed in the despair of its existence. Horror possessed him to know that such pain could abide in the world, but any pity he might have felt was extinguished as the arowl's teeth slashed toward Marshal's throat.

Bennek forced his own horror outward, into its mind, and it recoiled. Its jaws snapped shut on empty air. At the same time, Bennek sensed the searing passage of a violent spell. A fierce white flame ignited in the heart of the beast, just as Kit swung his sword to lop off its lifeless head.

Bennek returned to himself, wiping away rain drops from his face. He heard the crackle of fire, the beat of horses' hooves, and in the distance a racket of howling and warbling and baying.

"More arowl are coming!" Lanyon told him as she gripped his shoulder.

"Was it *your* fire spell?"

"No! It was the sorcerer's!"

"His name is Aidin."

"I have never heard that name. But he is skilled. He has destroyed all the arowl that came with him, even the dire wolf—"

"All of them?"

"I think so, but many more are coming. Maybe all those that were summoned south in the stampede."

Picking up his bow, Bennek looked out over the rocks. Despite the dribbling rain, fire moved through the grove where Marshal had been hidden. A second circle of angry flames burned in a thicket just south of his position, and a third fire burned across the meadow. He could see no arowl. But the sorcerer and his two men cantered closer.

"Lanyon, I don't know what to do. I don't know if they are friends or foes."

She fitted an arrow to her bowstring. "I wonder how far away the talisman can be sensed?"

"You think that's why they've come?"

"They are not here by chance."

Bennek nodded. "I will protect you."

His words were soft, almost lost within the patter of the rain. The oncoming riders could not have heard him. Yet as Bennek spoke, the sorcerer looked up—and then he turned his horse, and sent it crashing through the thickets and up the slope until he reached the foot of the rock outcropping where Bennek and Lanyon were hidden.

He reined in his horse. Then he called out in a wounded, raspy voice, "Lanyon! The beasts of Siddél come behind us. I called them off once before and lured them south. We killed many in your defense! But those that are left have tasted blood and will not give way. There is no time to be timid. We must draw together or none will live."

Lanyon turned to Bennek in bewilderment. "He speaks of that day the arowl stampeded south—yet I know of no one named Aidin."

"It must be he sees into your mind . . . or into mine?"

"Stand with me," she pleaded.

Bennek did not hesitate. They arose together. Both held their bows at full draw, arrows aimed at the sorcerer's heart. Bennek tried to make out a face beneath the shadow cast by the sorcerer's hood, but all he could see was the curve of a nose and a rough complexion.

"Who are you that knows me?" Lanyon asked. "How is it you command the arowl?"

When the sorcerer answered, his wounded voice sounded puzzled, "Are you truly confounded?" Pulling back his hood, he exposed a face that must once have been beautiful but was now weathered and horribly scarred.

So great was Lanyon's shock that her grip on the bow slipped. The arrow spun away into the wet rocks. Her face contorted. She doubled over as if she had been hit in the gut. For a moment she did not seem able to breathe. Then she screamed. An incoherent noise, a protest of primal rage and terror. The same scream Bennek's mother had uttered when she fell to the arowl. Heat rushed through him as thunder rumbled in the distance. "*Lanyon!*"

Bow in hand, she turned and fled, scrambling deeper into the rocks, carrying the talisman in its new case across her back. Bennek started after her. But then, from the corner of his eye, he saw Aidin turn his horse to give chase around the hillside and suddenly he knew what he must do.

He could not shoot the sorcerer. The people did not slay the people. So instead, still holding his bow and with his pack on his back, he leaped from the rocks, launching himself at the sorcerer.

Warning cries went up from the two warriors, but there was no time for Aidin to make a defense. Bennek struck him hard, knocking him from the saddle, but they tumbled as they fell and Bennek hit the ground first.

Time skipped.

Next he knew Kit was crouched beside him, breathing hard and shaking his shoulder. "Bennek! Bennek, wake up! I know you are not dead. I think the sorcerer stunned you."

Bennek blinked against the rain that dribbled in his eyes. Rain fell steadily, but it had not put out the fires yet. "Where did he go?" he wheezed.

Dry weeds burned mere steps away. Heat billowed over him, contrasting sharply with the cold splashes of raindrops. The flames spoke in a low, rushing, sizzling voice that did nothing to disguise a chorus of yammering howls resounding against the rocks.

"Come on!" Kit urged, hauling Bennek to a sitting position. "Get up. Clear your head. You must use Samoket's gift. The arowl are upon us and Marshal is alone among the trees."

"But the sorcerer . . . he knew Lanyon—"

"Do it now, Bennek, before the arowl find him."

The smoky flames crept closer as Bennek closed his eyes. He had hardly brushed the Mere when he said to Kit, "There is one stalking us a few steps behind you." He felt Kit move away, but he did not look.

He turned in the Fourth Way. His awareness leaped outward. At once he perceived Marshal, and it was as Kit said, he was alone within a grove of young trees that grew so close together there was hardly room for him to slip between them—but the arowl that pursued him were hampered too. Marshal held them off with just a knife, but they had him surrounded. It wouldn't be long before they grew bold and closed in.

Bennek came among them, a ghost bearing the rage of the people. The arowl felt his anger and quailed. Their excited baying transformed to fearful yips and uncertain whines. They fell back, leaving Marshal free for precious seconds. He slipped out of the grove and raced toward the rocks. But as he ran, another pack coming in from the east caught sight of him. Bennek haunted these next, sending his will among them, and they too fell back.

"Wake up!" Kit screamed.

Bennek felt himself hauled by his armpits. He returned from the Mere to find flames licking his boots, and fire dancing in smoky spirals in the brush. "Where's my bow?" He hunted for it, and almost stumbled over the small arowl Kit had just killed.

Kit found Bennek's bow first and handed it to him. "Where is Marshal?"

"You didn't see him?"

"No."

"He was running this way. He must have gone around the rocks."

"Come on, then," Kit said. "We'll find him when we climb up. Hurry. If this rain keeps up, the fires will be put out, and then nothing will stand between us and the arowl."

# 15

Lanyon had looked on the face of a dead man and panicked. It was not the sorcerer Aidin's scarred and weathered face that had sent her fleeing into the rocks. There *was* no Aidin. Aidin was a lie. The sorcerer behind the disfiguring scars was Édan. Her lover, her husband—137 years dead—a ghost made flesh. He could not still be within the world. He could not.

And yet, hadn't the mist warned her it was so? Days ago along the riverbank, whispering a haunting message: *He is coming. He is coming.*

Lanyon had thought the warning referred to Pantheren. She knew now the mist had feared Édan.

And still it made no sense to her.

She fled into the rocks where the horses could not follow. She had no plan, no destination. Her mind was in tumult. How could Édan be alive? And more improbable still, why would he choose to ride with the arowl—Siddél's hated beasts—that had killed his father and his grandfather? Édan had spent his life crusading against the blasphemy of the arowl's existence. He had used his sorcery to turn them against each other, and he had burned the pits where they were made.

He had believed he could defeat Siddél.

He had used the fire spell to slaughter such beasts as those he now brought with him.

And more arowl were coming. Many, many more. Lanyon heard their clamor as she ran and knew she could never outrun them all.

Reason tried to reassert itself. Édan might be able to defeat these arowl if he had her help, along with that of Pantheren, Marshal, Kit, Bennek, and his own two men.

But Lanyon rejected this thought and kept going, because she knew why Édan had come and what he wanted. And despite all, she swore to herself she would not let him have it. Pantheren had said it was Édan's task to slay Siddél, but Pantheren did not know what had happened that night.

Lanyon knew, but she had not told it all, not to Jahallon or to Pantheren or to anyone because Édan was dead and the truth did not matter anymore. It did not matter because *Édan was dead.*

Through a thin veil of rain, she glimpsed him in the rocks below. He had abandoned his horse to climb the rough terrain. He saw her and called out to her, "Lanyon, stop!"

She ducked past a wall of rock, to find herself in a damp, grassy hollow just below the hilltop.

What had he become?

*What had he been?*

It was not his task anymore.

She had only one arrow, but that one was enough.

As quickly as she could, she unstrapped the talisman and removed it from its case. She set it to the bowstring, just as he came around the rocks.

"Stop!" she told him. "Come no closer."

"Lanyon!"

She did not draw the bow, but held it poised in her hands. "What are you? Who are you?"

"You know me, Lanyon."

"No! Édan is dead. I saw him die."

"You mistook it! I should have died, but Siddél would not allow it."

"What did the monster do? Slip a fragment of his soul inside you? You must be his creation now."

"What madness is on you, Lanyon, to speak to me thus? Would you say such words to Jahallon? You cannot imagine what I have endured!"

She raised the bow, and drew it. "Do not tell it to me! I do not care."

His astonishment was plain, but it became dismay when he saw what arrow she had aimed at his heart.

"Yes," Lanyon told him. "It's a wicked thing, and I guided its flight when it killed you once before."

Then he thought he understood her. "You think I want revenge. Lanyon, it is not so. I know what happened that night. It was not your fault. You only did as I told you. In the smoke and the darkness there was no way for you to know. Be at peace."

"Be at peace? Do you think I have forgotten what you did that night?"

"I gave up all that I love! For the good of the people. To end this war. To bring down Siddél."

"Ashes!" she cried. "It is all ashes. Our children are dead for your vanity, Édan, and all those others who were slaughtered when the Citadel was broken. You thought it was given to you to destroy the monster, so you summoned him. You prepared the way. Jahallon told me there was no guard on the wall that night. No one on watch. No one to give us warning when—"

A deafening thunderclap resounded above them and she recoiled. The smattering rain became a torrent whipped sideways by a sudden gale, while out of the clouds a monstrous voice roared, "*What trickster has deceived my arowl?*"

Even as Lanyon shrank against the meager shelter of the rock wall, her astonished gaze turned skyward to see the Inyomere Siddél. He loomed above the hilltop, suspended amid a swirl of black clouds. A great, glowering, man-like form that bent low to search the land below. Lightning crackled along his limbs and his hair burned with blue flame. "*Who dares to trespass in the guarded lands?*"

In her shock, she forgot Édan. Siddél was all. More than chance that he should come down from his cloud fields now, when she had the talisman nocked and ready in her bow.

She raised her aim skyward and picked out the spell's path through the Mere. But then Édan was beside her. He seized the bow, wrenching it down as she let the arrow fly. The spell skewed from its path, and the cursed arrow spun uselessly away over the rocks.

Lanyon watched it go and all hope left her. Against the wind and the drumming rain her voice rose in a wail of despair. She cried out, "What have you done? What have you done?"

Édan answered her, though she did not understand the meaning of his words, "You have taken enough from me already. It is not for you to become the storm!"

Siddél espied them. He cried out, "Édan the trickster thief! Did I not leave you imprisoned in Nendaganon? And so you should be still! And will!"

Édan looked on the Inyomere with a malice Lanyon had never witnessed in him before, but his hatred could not protect him. Lightning leaped from Siddél's monstrous hand. It struck Édan in the chest with such force that he was lifted off his feet and thrown limp against the rocks on the other side of the hollow.

Siddél descended to the ground. Lanyon huddled against the stone, a scant arm's reach from the Inyomere of black cloud and fire, standing three times the height of a man. He scowled at her, lightning dancing on his brow, though he spoke to her gently, "Petty spirit! Do not allow Édan the Trickster to beguile you. There is no place for the people in the Wild."

Édan stirred weakly and a moan escaped him. Siddél heard it and leaped on him. The monster landed on Édan's chest with such force that Lanyon heard bones snap. Blood gushed into Édan's mouth and streamed from his nose and eyes. Siddél saw it and laughed. "Back to the pits," he said, "where you will stay until this war is ended."

He bent as if to pick up Édan's broken body, but at that moment an arrow hissed from the rocks overhead. It struck the monster in the back just below the shoulder blade, reaching deep to where his heart should be. Siddél roared and leaped into the clouds as a second arrow pursued him.

Lanyon followed the path of that arrow back, and saw Pantheren standing on the rocks above her. He drew his bow, sending a third arrow up into the clouds to convince Siddél he was not safe even there—and at this assault the wounded Inyomere turned and fled.

With his departure, the wind calmed and the rain eased to an uncertain patter, but the changing weather brought no comfort, for the cries of the arowl pack were now close and joyous.

Pantheren jumped down from the rocks. "Are you hurt?" he asked Lanyon.

"No."

He went to gaze at Édan's crushed body, and Lanyon went with him.

Édan was dead. She could not doubt it. Blood pooled in his mouth and in the hollows of his eyes and no breath stirred on his lips—and yet his skin was not burnt from the lightning, and his chest was not crushed.

"Lanyon!" Bennek called from the rocks below.

Relief overcame her at this proof he was still alive. She turned and leaned out over the rocks and looked down. "Bennek! We are here!"

He came running with Kina at his heels and Marshal and Kit just behind. "Lanyon! Are you all right? We saw the terrible storm and—" He stumbled over Édan's body. Stopped in shock to stare. Then he turned an uncertain gaze on her. "Did you . . . ?"

"No. It was Siddél."

"Speak, Lanyon," Pantheren said. "What has happened here?"

She nudged Édan's body with the toe of her shoe to be sure. "A monster has slain a monster."

"You speak thus? But I heard Siddél name him! Was the Inyomere mistaken? Or is this Édan?"

"It is him," she answered, giving way to bitterness. "Now I have seen him die twice."

"And grieved once? Or not at all?"

"Not for him! Not then. Not now. He has doomed us, just as he did in the Citadel. He wrecked my shot! He allowed Siddél to live and now the fatal arrow is lost and all the arowl of Samokea come to feed on us."

Marshal stepped past Bennek, his face flush with exertion. Bloodstains glistened on his coat. "I do not understand how this could be Édan, and there is no time now to make it out, but take heart! We are not alone. I have seen a small company of eleven men on horseback. They pursue the arowl and harry them, keeping them in doubt."

"Likely more of Édan's men," Pantheren guessed. He went to look.

Through the thinning skeins of smoke Pantheren saw only five horsemen, not eleven, engaged in a running battle with at least fifteen arowl. Frustration swept over him. He had been wrong. These were not Édan's men. He told the others, "These are men of Habaddon."

Pantheren knew he should be grateful they had come. Their help was desperately needed. Yet he regretted their presence. He did not want them to end their lives here. They should not *be* here—and they would not have come if he had succeeded in bringing Lanyon to Habaddon. He felt sure of that. But it could not be undone.

"There is Jakurian, out in front," he said. "And beside him, Bahir. I think Jahallon knew of this gathering of arowl and sent a company to support us—but now they are hard-pressed."

"There are more than these five," Marshal said. He pointed east. "Some have gone into that grove where these riders are headed."

As if to prove it, a volley of arrows flew from the trees. Many of the pursuing arowl fell—but the pack had its own hidden allies. From the foot of the hill on which they stood, an answering volley took flight and at least one arrow found its target, sending a man tumbling from his horse.

The horse fled to join its companions within the trees, but one of the warriors turned back, taking up his fallen companion. More arrows hissed around them as they raced to the shelter of the grove. All the while, the lamentations of a hundred or more arowl reverberated in the thickets and trees to the south of the hill.

"Do we stand here and watch?" Kit demanded angrily. "Or do

we help these men? Or do we mean to abandon them and go on while the attention of the arowl is turned from us?"

Lanyon answered him sharply, "We cannot go on. The talisman is lost and we cannot leave here until it's found again."

This answer induced in Kit a cold smile of satisfaction. "Well then, we must fight. I like our chances better anyway if we slaughter these arowl now, then if we let them hunt us later . . . although my arrows are nearly gone."

"Take half of mine," Pantheren said. "Lanyon, you must come with us until we find some defensible place—"

"I will follow when I have found the talisman."

"I cannot leave you here undefended."

"Then leave someone with me. War Father, we cannot risk some were-beast finding it, or one of those warriors who rode here with Édan."

Bennek stepped forward. "I will help you find it."

But Marshal objected. "Bennek, the arowl are many and your talents are better used in the battle below. Go with Kit and Pantheren. I'll stay with Lanyon, and when we have found the arrow, we'll join you."

Pantheren was not pleased, but time was short. "Stay hidden," he warned them. "And we will do all we can to keep the arowl from climbing this hill." He called softly to Kina and set off, with Kit close behind.

Bennek lingered a little longer. To Marshal he said, "The two who rode with"—his uneasy gaze turned to the corpse—"with *him* . . . they retreated north when Siddél came, but now they make their way back."

"We will be wary," Marshal assured him.

Bennek looked at Lanyon. "I'm sorry I did not stop him from following you. It was enough that you feared him. I should not have shown him any mercy."

"Bennek, it's never wrong to listen to your heart."

He shook his head. "My heart is confused." Then he was away, bounding down the hill after Pantheren.

Pantheren crept beneath dripping trees and over moss-covered rocks, with Kit following just steps behind him. When he spied a trio of were-beasts in the thickets below, he held up a hand to stop.

From Kit, a slight bloodthirsty smile. Bennek appeared behind him. They spread out a little. Pantheren nocked an arrow and said, very softly, "*Now.*"

All three fired simultaneously, and then fired again.

The arowl had not suspected an attack from above. The three were-beasts fell, but many smaller arowl that they had not seen before now sprang up, and in a panic they fled into the meadow—where they met a fresh onslaught of arrows from the men of Habaddon. None of the beasts escaped.

"A good beginning," Kit said in satisfaction.

"But just the beginning," Pantheren replied, knowing the vanquished pack was no more than a forward party. By far the greater number of arowl bided in the forest to the south, crying out in their hunger and their despair.

Still, a respite had been won. They hurried to retrieve their arrows. Then they gathered at the edge of the thickets as the warrior Jakurian rode over to meet them.

Pantheren and Jakurian knew each other well. Jakurian was the youngest child of Jahallon's present wife, Nurea of Clan Samoket, though he was no youth. He had thirty-two years in the world, almost half of those on the battlefield. Like any fighting man his age, he had witnessed tragedy, endured pain, and faced the loss of close friends. But through it all, Jakurian had held onto his sunny disposition, and he was well-loved for it.

Now, despite the hardships of the day, he jumped down from his horse with a triumphant grin. "Pantheren! My teacher and my captain! It's a joy to meet you in this unmapped land."

"Though not all unexpected?" Pantheren asked him as they clasped hands, the rain falling again in a slow but steady drizzle.

"It's true we are here looking for you," Jakurian admitted. "You were expected in Habaddon. When you did not come, we grew worried. And then a scout reported having seen smoke rising near the River Talahnon. We wondered if you had gone that way, perhaps persuaded to try for Ohtangia instead of Habaddon?"

"Ah, so you thought me bewitched?" Pantheren asked with some amusement.

Jakurian shrugged. "Bewitched or waylaid. In either circumstance, we meant to find you. We looked first for the source of the smoke, and found a burnt hillside and the remains of a battle. And then we let ourselves be distracted. From that hilltop we looked north, and saw in the distance three men on horseback, and running with them a pack of arowl! We could hardly believe our eyes. I sent two men back to Habaddon with the news."

"And then you followed these strangers?"

"Did we have a choice? What sort of men would ally themselves with arowl? And yet the beasts are their enemies too." He half-turned, and gestured to the south. "This great pack was once even larger, but these men contrived to use fire against it. They killed many, while passing through the horde unscathed. I cannot say the same for my own company. We have lost two men."

"I am sorry for it."

"At least we have found you . . . though I don't understand why you are here, so deep in Samokea."

Pantheren answered this sharply, "I go where my duty takes me."

"I meant no censure—"

"And you have come too late to collect your quarry. I think there was only one among the three who could command the beasts. He was called Aidin by his men—"

"Aidin . . . ? I have heard that name."

"I've heard it too," Pantheren said. "Some years ago Jahallon sent an emissary to a new settlement in Ohtangia—"

"—a settlement founded by Aidin of Clan Samoket," Jakurian finished for him. "I remember it. But there was a mystery to it. No emissary since has found the way back to Aidin's fort, and it's rumored he is a sorcerer."

Pantheren said, "If it's the same man, there is no doubt of that. His tale is strange and bitter, but he is dead now. Siddél has seen to it. The monster came this day to assert that no one should command the arowl but him."

Jakurian shook his head in wonder. "Siddél! I heard his thunder, though I thought he only celebrated this great gathering of beasts. But what of the woman, Lanyon Kyramanthes? Is she still with you?"

"Should I have gone on without her? She is here, and so far she is safe, but this day is full of peril."

"That I well know." Jakurian's gaze turned curiously to Kit and Bennek. "Ah, War Father, how I long to hear all your story, not least how you gathered allies in an empty land, but these arowl are unlikely to be so patient."

"We need to kill them," Pantheren agreed. "*All* of them. Our journey has just begun and I do not want these beasts howling down our trail."

Lanyon stood again in the precise place she'd been when she aimed the talisman at Siddél. She recalled how it had looked soaring out of sight over the rocks. She described its path to Marshal, and together they went to look.

Marshal searched the rain-soaked thickets, looking for the gleam of steel, while Lanyon resolved to search the Mere.

She sat cross-legged, focusing her mind on the Fourth Way. Her vision did not reach far within the spirit-world, but even so she sensed the presence of not one, but two dire spells.

The talisman she knew, for she was accustomed to its presence, but the second spell was unknown to her. It felt dark and dreadful, a great spirit-beast bearing a terrible gravity that would surely crush her if she dared disturb it. It did not want to be disturbed. It *pushed* at her, forcing her to look away. She complied at once. Perhaps this wicked spell had a name, but she could not hear it. She didn't want to know it. She fled the Mere, shuddering as she opened her eyes amid the drip of rain and the gloomy shadows of the thickets.

Drawing a shaky breath, she tried to forget what she had seen. "Marshal?"

His search had taken him farther down the hill, but he returned at her call. "Let's look around here. The talisman is very close."

She let herself be guided by the lure of its wicked presence, but Marshal spotted it first, nearly buried in the soggy leaf litter. Lanyon took it, her hands shaking in relief as she used the wet hem of her coat to wipe it clean.

She and Marshal were both soaked through, their fingers pale and shriveled, but there was nothing to be done for it. "Would that we could summon Siddél again," she said in bitterness, "without Édan to spoil the shot."

Marshal replied with quiet confidence, "We will find him at the Storm Lair, if we do not find him first along the way."

Lanyon returned the talisman to the case the Snow Chanter had made for it. Then Marshal gave her two of his remaining arrows: "In case the arowl discover us," he explained.

They set out through the thickets to find their companions. They had not gone far when they heard the crackling, crunching noise of some large and thoughtless creature pushing past brittle branches—and then they heard the snort of a horse. Both dropped to a crouch behind a screen of twigs.

From there they could look up the slope to see three horses tethered where the thicket gave way to grass. One neighed a soft greeting as the two gray-haired warriors came into view, making a swift but careful retreat from the hilltop. Between them they carried the limp and bloody corpse of Édan.

When the pair reached their horses, one took over the task of holding Édan's body, while the other climbed into the saddle. The horse shuddered and pranced, unsettled by the scent of so much blood, but the rider spoke to it soothingly as he bent low to help his companion lift the corpse. As soon as he had Édan's remains cradled in his arms, he set out. The second man fetched the other two horses and, mounting one, he followed after his companion.

They made their way down the hill, passing close to where

Lanyon and Marshal were hidden, and as they went by, Lanyon saw Édan's head turn. That motion might have been caused by the jolting stride of the horse, but she could make no such excuse for the sudden, darting movement of Édan's eyes as he looked directly at her, nor could she explain the way his hand rose on its own to grip the horse's mane.

# 16

Jakurian had set out with fourteen men, but of these, two had been sent back to Habaddon and two had been lost in battle with the arowl. Two more were wounded and could no longer fight from horseback. Pantheren took one of the riderless horses, sending the two wounded men with Kit and Bennek to make a stand in the rocks overlooking the meadow.

The rain persisted in a half-hearted drizzle as the company fought a swift skirmish with a pack of some twenty arowl that dared to enter the meadow.

Never before had Kit and Bennek seen combat from horseback. They watched the fighting with fascination, but Bennek still remembered to slip at times into the Mere. Before long, he told Kit, "Marshal and Lanyon are looking for us."

"Then they have found the talisman."

Kit crept into the rocks to meet them. He showed them the way down.

Lanyon went at once to Bennek. "Did you watch the two who rode with the sorcerer? Do you know where they went?"

"To the hilltop. They lifted up his body and took it away."

Anxiously, she asked, "Could you see him, Bennek? Even though he was dead?"

"I could," Bennek realized. "He was no longer hidden in his glamour. But . . . if his spirit was gone, what was I seeing?"

Lanyon looked panicky. "Where did they go? Do you know?"

"East into the grasslands. They are riding in the cut of a dry stream, hunched low to hide their presence. I think they hope to slip away before the arowl take notice."

Nodding, she turned to look out on the meadow where Jakurian's men stood scattered at the edge of the trees, all dismounted, resting their horses. Not a single arowl could be seen, though their discontented mewling, growling, and barking filled the air.

"Where are the beasts?" Lanyon asked.

The Habaddon man, Bahir, answered her. "They hide within the trees to the south."

The arrow that had knocked Bahir from his horse had left his shoulder badly torn. His right arm was now bound against his chest, and the pain of his wound could be read in his face. Even so, he gripped a sword in his left hand and kept a close watch on the land all around.

He told Lanyon, "The beasts don't lack for numbers, but they are exhausted by their run north, and chastened at their losses."

"Surely their hunger will overcome their fear?"

"When they are rested."

"We can't allow them to rest," Kit said. "We need to go after them. Hunt them one by one."

Bahir shook his head. "They are too many to pursue on foot. Once among the trees they would overwhelm us. We must draw them out."

"If it comes to it, we can wait till nightfall," Bennek suggested. "After dark they will be slow."

Marshal used his sleeve to wipe the rain from his face. "They are many, Bennek, and our count of arrows is low. It would be close-combat the night long, and the weather is against us."

Kaliel, the second Habaddon man, held a position with bow in hand. He gazed out over the meadow, though he was feverish from the rending bite of a were-wolf that had torn his calf and thigh. "I think a decision has been made," he said. "Pantheren comes, with Jakurian behind him."

The two men cantered their horses up to the burnt thicket at the base of the rock outcropping. "Bennek!" Pantheren called out.

Bennek leaned over the edge, hoping to be given some interesting task.

"Bennek, we grow weary of waiting for the beasts to find their nerve. I would have you use Samoket's gift to bewitch them, as I have heard you can do these many days."

"Sir, it is fear that keeps the arowl hidden. If I panic them more, it will drive them off and delay the battle for hours, until their hunger brings them back again."

Pantheren raised a hand for patience. "I would have you bewitch them with a different spirit, Bennek. Can you kindle a fire in their corrupt hearts that will embolden them? Is that something you can do? Feed their hunger? Persuade them to take the field?"

Bennek felt all eyes on him, but in particular he felt the weight of Jakurian's doubtful gaze, so he took care to answer in a clear voice. "I do not know, sir. I have never before had need to make the arowl more fierce."

"Will you try?" Pantheren pressed.

Bennek looked to Marshal for approval and received a quick nod. "I will try, sir."

"Good! But that is not all I ask of you. When the arowl are on the field, when they have come out to menace us, I want them confounded. Let them know your wrath. Let fear take them. Can you do that?"

"Sir, that is an easy thing, though it will take time." He glanced cautiously at Marshal, but went on anyway. "All the time I work this trick I cannot hunt. I will make no kills."

"The kills we make will be in your name."

"That is not the same, sir."

Jakurian grinned, but Pantheren looked annoyed. "Bennek. We are all weary, wet, and cold. We need to finish this battle quickly. Each of us must serve as he is best suited and only you can confound the arowl."

"He'll do it," Marshal said, looking down to where the two captains sat their horses.

Bennek gave up the argument. "As you wish, sir. Make ready." He dropped behind the rocks, gloomy at his lot.

Kit crouched beside him. "Can you do this thing?"

"I don't know. I don't possess a blood hunger. So how can I call this desire from among the arowl?"

"You've rarely known fear or panic either," Marshal pointed out, "but you lead the arowl to them easily enough. Just do it, Bennek. You know you can."

Still thinking on it, Bennek settled down with his back against the wet stone. His spear he placed at his right hand and his bow he laid at his left, so that he would be ready if the arowl overran the rocks.

"I will watch over you," Marshal promised.

"You may become distracted." It was then Bennek noticed Bahir and Kaliel, and the wary way they watched him.

"Are you a sorcerer?" Bahir asked.

"He has a talent that has come down to him from Samoket," Marshal said quickly, "but that is all."

Bennek heard caution in his brother's voice and wondered at it, but Marshal left no time for questions.

"Make ready, Bennek. The men of Habaddon are waiting."

He nodded and, closing his eyes, he turned in the Fourth Way.

At Jakurian's order, the horsemen moved out onto the meadow. They did not have to wait long for the arowl. Horses snorted and some reared as the restive, mewling chatter of the beasts abruptly shifted into a blood-thirsty chorus of howls—a barbarous song that spread through the forest until it seemed the trees themselves were howling.

The Habaddon men exclaimed in astonishment. Jakurian, his mouth wide in wonder, turned to Pantheren. "It is exactly as you commanded!"

Pantheren drew his sword. Speaking softly, he warned Jakurian, "Take heed. This is the same skill Édan possessed when he captained the armies of Samokea."

Movement beneath the trees. A chaos of hideous shapes. Jakurian stood in his stirrups and shouted to his men. "Make ready! They are coming!"

Kina, who had been waiting patiently among the horses, threw back her head and offered up her own joyous howl as the arowl swarmed into the open. They numbered ninety or more, tongues lolling in their lust for the blood of men and horses.

"Stand firm," Jakurian warned. "Stand firm . . ." He waited until the last of the pack had run well clear of the trees. "Ride now! Surround them!"

The horsemen split into two lines, racing around the huge pack, hemming it in and driving the beasts toward the rocks. Howls of rage erupted, and arrows flew from both sides.

"Now Bennek!" Pantheren bellowed above the chaos. "Turn them now!"

At this command, the pack's battle-fury began to peel away. One by one, each beast remembered its weariness. The intoxicating blood hunger that had driven them from the trees became a crippling emptiness in the gut. The were-wolves shrieked their despair, the were-bears lowed, and the four-footed arowl mewed and cried.

Those closest to the trees cut past the horsemen, racing back to that refuge. But most scattered, fleeing this way and that, while the horsemen rode them down, one by one.

Several ran toward the rocks. A poor decision. Instead of a spear or sword, they met death in a hail of arrows.

Bennek was gone, deep into the Mere. Never before had it fallen to him to beguile so many arowl, and to confound their minds first one way and then another. There were too many for him to work his will on all at once, so he went from one to the next to the next until he forgot himself, and for a time it seemed to him that he had always been an ethereal creature of menace and doom haunting the meadow and the open plain. He did not remember to look behind the hill where he sheltered.

It happened that a small pack of arowl had wandered around that hill, following the trail of Édan's men until they heard the howls of blood-hunger. Then they turned back. Just six in number, but two were great dire wolves, larger than horses, and no one knew they were there.

Kina caught the scent first. With the rain still falling, she left the meadow, bounding through the wet ashes of a burnt thicket before leaping into the rocks.

Marshal saw her coming. He and Kaliel had taken positions on either side of Bennek, who still sat with his back against the stone, his youthful face fixed in an expression of deep concentration.

As the dog leaped past him, Marshal stood up in alarm. He turned to follow her with his gaze and saw movement above. "Kit! Kaliel! Lanyon! Behind us! Bennek—wake up now!"

He shook Bennek hard by the shoulder, but didn't stay to see if he awoke. No time for it, as a great dire wolf came leaping down the hillside with smaller arowl around it.

Marshal thought the dire wolf must be the same beast he had seen on the prairie three days before, with white slashes on its shoulders, a wound at its neck, and a length of chain swinging from its collar. He drew his sword, shouting, "I'll stop the wolf. Take care of the other beasts!"

Lanyon set her last arrow against her bowstring and launched it at a horned were-beast as it charged into the narrow space where they sheltered in the rocks. The arrow struck deep in its chest, but the beast kept coming, answering her assault with a swinging sword. She ducked the whooshing blade and retreated, summoning the fire spell as Kit stepped in. He hammered his sword against the back of the were-beast's neck, just as the white-hot spell ignited in its heart, and it collapsed.

Like Lanyon, Kaliel too had used his last arrow, but he still had a spear. Despite blood loss and fever, he used it to hold off two tracking arowl.

Bahir faced a clawed beast whose wide jaws displayed hundreds of needle teeth stained green by the poison of its drool. With his back to a rock, he held it off in a desperate one-handed contest.

Kina bypassed all these lesser arowl. Like Marshal, her chosen prey was the dire wolf. She reached it first. With a ferocious snarl she threw herself at the wolf's wounded throat, tearing fur and flesh. As soon as she leaped away, Marshal attacked, thrusting his sword up and into the wolf's throat just in front of the collar, moving nimbly aside as a fountain of blood showered the rocks. The wolf staggered several steps, then collapsed in a thrashing heap—revealing a second wolf behind it.

Like its fallen pack mate, this one wore a collar, but its coat was night-black—a stark contrast to the white slashes scarring its shoulders. It leaped over its dead companion, landing on the rocks just above the fray.

Scant seconds had passed since the melee began. Bennek still sat on the ground, bleary from his trance, gazing in confusion at the dire wolf that glowered down at him.

"Bennek run!" Marshal screamed.

Bennek came to life at his shout. He seized his spear, scrambling to get up as the dire wolf leaped. But he'd made it only halfway to his feet when the wolf impaled itself on his spear. The spearhead disappeared into its chest, but the shaft kicked back against rock and snapped, throwing Bennek off-balance. He stumbled, catching his heel as the weight of the wolf slammed against him. There was not even time to be afraid.

The dire wolf heard the sound of bone breaking. It felt its prey go limp. The triumph of its hunger drove away all awareness of its own wound and it opened its jaws to rend its prey with massive fangs—until a white-hot pain ignited in its throat. It reared back, fire billowing from its open maw. Then it went berserk.

It plunged witlessly, shaking its head and biting at stone in a frantic effort to fight back against an attacker it could not reach.

Bahir had just finished off the needle-toothed arowl. He saw the dire wolf in its death throes and wisely retreated into the rocks. Kaliel was almost trampled. Then Kit stepped in. He plunged his sword into the dire wolf's side, sinking it to its hilt, and the tormented beast collapsed.

# 17

Marshal bounded down from the rocks, skirting the massive carcass of the dire wolf to reach his brother. Kit, on his knees beside Bennek, looked up with tearful eyes. Lanyon crouched at Bennek's other side, weeping, and Marshal thought the sound of it would rend his heart.

Bennek was a crumpled thing. He lay at the base of the rock, his waxen face turned to the rain, his half-open eyes focused on nothing, though every few seconds he blinked. Scarlet blood dripped from his nose and the corner of his mouth. More blood soaked his trousers just where his leg bent at an impossible angle above the right knee. Horror clutched at Marshal when he saw it.

Kit read his expression. He stood with a snarl and stepped away, to stand with shoulders hunched and a hand over his eyes.

Marshal went to him, whispering, "I don't know what to do. I have never seen such injuries before."

A heavy hand gripped his shoulder. He looked around to see the Habaddon warrior, Bahir, whose right arm was bound up in a sling.

"Speak to your brother," Bahir urged. "Give him the comfort of your presence, but don't move him yet."

Bahir circled around to Lanyon. Crouching beside her, he said, "Come. Step away for a bit. It does him no good to hear your despair."

He took her away, leaving Bennek alone until Marshal knelt beside him. He touched his brother's cheek. "Bennek? Bennek do you hear me?"

Bennek's chin moved in the slightest of nods, but he didn't speak or shift his fixed gaze.

"We'll take care of you, Bennek. We'll keep you safe."

Pantheren came climbing up from the meadow, breathing hard in his haste. "Let me see him."

Marshal stood and stepped aside. As he did, his gaze passed over the meadow and with astonishment, he realized the battle had ended. Arowl carcasses lay strewn across the muddy grass. Men moved among them, assuring all were truly dead. Only a single man lay on the ground. Jakurian knelt, tending him.

Marshal looked again at Bennek. Pantheren knelt at his side, examining him, gently probing the back of his skull, and then his chest and his arms.

"I saw the wolf fall on him," Pantheren said. "His head struck the rock. A harsh blow. Only time will tell the cost of that. And some of his ribs are broken, though I think his lungs were spared."

Drawing his knife, Pantheren used it to cut open Bennek's blood-soaked trouser leg. He folded back the cloth, revealing a white gleam of bone deep within torn flesh. Fear erupted in a hot flush across Marshal's skin. Already the leg had begun to swell.

Pantheren looked up at him. "Get a blanket and lay it on the ground. There's room enough here to work. You'll help me wash his wound and set his leg. Then I'll teach you how to sew up his torn flesh." He barked out orders to the men on the field. "Sanno! This warrior cannot ride. I'll need you to make a litter. Fen, you will get me a splint. Kit!"

Kit came, his cheeks wet with tears.

"Take the gray horse I was using and go back to Medesh. See if that house is still open to us. Take Lanyon with you—"

He turned to look for her, but Bahir had taken her away into the rocks. Pantheren went after them, and found her kneeling on the ground, still weeping. Bahir shook his head, saying, "This day has been too much for her."

"And still it is not done." Pantheren knelt at her side. "Lanyon, put aside your despair. Bennek yet lives and there is much you can do for him and these other men."

She looked up at him, and through her tears she asked in bitterness, "Do you trust me to do it? For all that I touch and all that I love soon turns to ashes."

"Do not think on it. You are a Kyramanthes woman. Your mother has taught you the ways of war and how to tend the wounded, and I need your help now. So save your tears, and pray that the Snow Chanter will give us shelter again this night."

Of all the descendants of Jahallon-the-Undying, the people of Kyramanthes had been most affected by the curse of Siddél. Through that heritage they gained some talents of the Inyomere, but Siddél's fiery nature also affected them, making them a rash and passionate people who gave little heed to danger. And they loved the Wild. Like the Inyomere, they could not bear to be parted from it. It became their way to live in tents, moving about in the vastness of Ohtangia, always at home wherever they were in that land.

By necessity the Kyramanthes had been builders too. They made many fortresses where they could retreat when the arowl came marauding. In those times when the men were away at war, the duty of defense rested solely with the women.

So from an early age every girl learned not only to read the histories and write the prayers, to glean food from the land and to fish, to cook and sew, but also to handle horses, to shoot a bow in hunting and in defense, and to tend the wounded.

Lanyon had learned some of the healer's arts from her mother, and more from Jahallon when she lived in his house. So she went with Kit on the sweat-stained gray horse to prepare for the wounded who would follow.

A misty rain fell, and the day had gone soft and quiet. The tired horse went slowly through the wet grass. So much had transpired since their departure from Medesh that it seemed to Lanyon the house of the Snow Chanter must lie at some great distance, but it was not so. Very soon they came upon the place where the trees stood tall at the edge of the plain. The stream ran from the forest, just as Lanyon remembered, but the house did not appear to them.

"We need to let the horse drink," Lanyon whispered, unwilling to speak of her disappointment.

Kit nodded. They slipped from the horse's back, and he led it to the stream. "We could cut boughs to make a shelter," he suggested.

"We may need to." Lanyon studied the forested slopes, but if there was any handy cave nearby, the trees hid it from her.

The horse lifted its head from the stream. Water dripped from its lips as it snorted, huffing air through its wide nostrils. Lanyon caught the scent too. *Woodsmoke!* She turned to look, hardly daring to hope—and there it was, the white house with sweeping red eaves and golden thatch, lovely within a veil of rain.

She ran to the door and opened it, but the Snow Chanter was not there. Kit hunted around the porch and behind the bathhouse but they could not find her.

"She may still come," he said.

"I hope that she can."

He helped her carry water and then he returned to the battleground. She built up the fire and set the water to warm. Then she checked the cabinets. Finding them all full again, she set food out on the table.

Before long, Kit came back, guiding the wounded—Kaliel and Bahir, along with Alhimbra, who had suffered a spear-thrust. All but Bennek, who could not ride a horse and had to be carried on a litter.

Pantheren walked in misty rain. Beside him, Jakurian led his horse, with the Habaddon men following on foot behind them.

The men had insisted on carrying Bennek's litter: "We owe him our lives. The arowl sorely out-numbered us. We survived only because he confounded them like Édan of old."

Marshal had been quick to correct them. "Bennek's gift came down to him from Samoket, *not* from Édan."

Now Marshal trudged beside the litter, grim and guilt-laden, clearly blaming himself for what had happened to his brother. The way Pantheren saw it, the Samokeän boys had long enjoyed an uncanny luck in the dangerous game they played with the arowl. But luck will change.

Kina, too, chose to stay close to Bennek, escorting him with her tail low. She was a young dog, but she'd been to war for two seasons now, and never before had Pantheren seen her so distraught over a wounded man.

Near noon, they approached the site of the cottage. The rain relented. The sun strove to peer past heavy clouds. Pantheren looked ahead, surprised to find he could see the little house from a distance, and even more surprised to see the Snow Chanter standing in the rain-wet field, waiting to greet them. The rain had not dampened her hair, and no mud showed on her white gown. Even her shoes were clean.

Jakurian looked up, saw her, saw what she was, and reached for his sword.

"No," Pantheren said, putting a restraining hand on his arm.

"She is Inyomere. We can expect only malice from her kind."

"Your mother is Samokeän," Pantheren reminded him. "See with her eyes."

Jakurian lowered his sword as a look of wonder came over him. "I know you! You are the Mother of Samokea, Tayeraisa the Snow Chanter . . . though I do not know how I know it, or how such a thing can be."

A puzzled murmur arose from the Habaddon men, and the litter bearers came to a stop.

The Snow Chanter studied Jakurian, her expression both curious and sad. "Your face I know well. It is so like the face of Samoket that I tremble in remembrance."

Pantheren said to her, "This is Jakurian, Blessed One. He is the son of Jahallon and of Nurea of Clan Samoket. So Samoket is his long-ago brother."

"Well met, Jakurian, though my heart is heavy this day." She approached the litter, and crouched beside Bennek. "Here lies my child who has redeemed and defended me, now grievously wounded."

"Can you help him, Blessed One?" Marshal pleaded.

Tayeraisa laid her hand against Bennek's cheek. He stirred at her touch. Pantheren thought he saw a blush of warmth in the boy's cheeks. But Tayeraisa told them, "It was Samoket's will that all should live or die in their turn. So I did not ever learn this mystery."

She stood up again and stepped away, just as Lanyon came running from the cottage. Heedless of the wet grass, Lanyon dropped to her knees beside Bennek and whispered his name. "Bennek, Bennek, do you still live? Show me that you live."

His eyes fluttered open and his gaze fixed on her—but only for a moment. "You must not leave us, Bennek. I beg you. Please stay with us a while yet."

The Snow Chanter took her hand. "Rise up, my Little Sister. There is not time to grieve, for the Long War has come to a dangerous tipping point."

Lanyon turned to her, wide-eyed, and Pantheren too found himself fearing what the Inyomere would say.

Tayeraisa's gaze took in all of them. "Hearken to me now, my Little Sister, my far sons. Hear me, warriors of Habaddon. My news is dire. On this day, before the sun rose, I was summoned by one who is great among my kind. He is called Jamu-karizen, though if his name is known to the people, I cannot say."

"It is known," Lanyon whispered.

Pantheren added warily, "It is known, but rarely spoken."

Among the Inyomere of the Wild, the petty Inyomere were most common: small, nameless spirits, confined to tiny realms, ignorant and uncaring of the larger land around them. Far fewer in number were those like the Snow Chanter and Siddél, who possessed a pervasive awareness of the Wild. They knew one another by name, and sometimes spoke together across the Expanse. Only a few had made the fate of the people their concern, but from the people all had learned the concepts of time and purpose and consequence.

Rarest of all were the fundamental spirits, like Jamu-karizen, remote from the people and unseen by them. The name of Jamu-karizen was known to the people only because the lesser Inyomere would speak now and then of He Who Held Up the Mountains. Jamu-karizen was weighty stone and dreadful time. He ruled the deep places, and could shake the very roots of the mountains.

The Snow Chanter told them, "It is within the power of Jamu-karizen to re-make the face of the Wild: to tear the mountains down or build them higher, to flood the coasts or raise them far above the reach of the ocean, or to shake Habaddon and Hallah and the sad ruins of the Citadel so that not one stone stands anymore atop another.

"Such has always been his power, but soon it may be his will.

"As I stood before him, even as Siddél brought his thunder here to threaten you, Jamu-karizen said to me, 'No more.' He will endure the weeping of the Wild no longer. He told me:

"*Once upon a time I believed the Long War would reveal the intent of the One who wakened us. If the people were meant to live within the Wild, they would overcome Siddél's abomination, but if they trespassed against the will of the One, they would be destroyed. So I waited and watched. For too long! The Wild can hardly endure its wounds. An end must be made.*"

The Snow Chanter looked at Lanyon. "Jamu-karizen knows who you are, Little Sister. He knows what you intend. I have prayed to him for time, that you may try. But if it falls to Jamu-karizen to end the Long War, I tell all of you now that it will not be ended in the people's favor."

"It is our purpose to end it," Lanyon protested. "It is our task. It should have ended this very day. I wanted to end it. I *will* end it. Far Mother, please, persuade him to wait."

"I will pray to him," the Snow Chanter promised. "But in the end he will make up his own mind."

Bennek was brought inside the cottage, his litter placed near the fire, though apart from the other wounded men. Then the battle-weary men dispersed to tend the horses and to bathe, leaving Lanyon alone with the wounded.

The fire crackled and popped, while on the stove a great pot of water murmured as it boiled. Lanyon took off her wet coat. Her boots she'd left outside. There was nothing she could do this day to soothe or satisfy Jamu-karizen, but there was much she could do for Bennek.

She had found dry blankets in the cabinets. She took one, and knelt beside Bennek. He lay still, his eyes closed. She touched his cheek, but he didn't respond. His breathing sounded ragged and shallow.

Fighting tears, Lanyon gingerly pulled back the damp blanket still tucked around him. The gold pendant he always wore gleamed in the firelight. Pantheren had cut away his clothes, using the soft, strong fabric of Bennek's shirt to bind his ribs. And he had set Bennek's leg, and stitched closed the wound made by the broken ends of bone, though scarlet blood still seeped through.

Lanyon covered Bennek with the dry blanket, listening to the click of Kina's toenails as the dog paced the porch, whining each time she passed the door.

For the next few minutes, she worked hanging up coats and blankets to dry. Then Kit came in, fresh from the bathhouse. He went to Bennek and sat cross-legged on the floor beside him, cupping his hand. "Does he look better?"

Lanyon knelt on Bennek's other side. "It's the firelight. It puts color in his cheeks, but his face is cold."

Kit sagged, miserable again. "Marshal said the Snow Chanter doesn't know any spell that will help."

"Tayeraisa is our beloved far mother, but she is not of the people."

"You are," Kit said, sitting up straight again and looking at her with keen eyes. He glanced at the other wounded men, but they were asleep. "Is there something you know to do for him?"

"It will take some time."

"I will help you."

She looked up at the sound of footsteps on the porch. The door opened, and Pantheren came in with Jakurian.

Lanyon had been surprised to learn that Jakurian was Jahallon's son, for Jahallon had taken no wife in all the many generations since Samoket's mother died. Until he met Nurea of Clan Samoket it had been the common belief of his people that he would never marry again.

"Lanyon, come," Pantheren said. "Jakurian would speak with you."

She stood and bowed to him, and he bowed to her in turn. "I have heard your story, Lanyon Kyramanthes, and I have seen your face before, in a painting that hangs within my father's keep."

"Jahallon said he made such paintings to help him remember the past."

"That is still his way. Lanyon, I thank you for tending my men."

"The people care for one another, War Father. It is our way."

Jakurian went to look at his wounded men on the other side of the fire, while Lanyon returned to Bennek. She knelt at the head of the litter.

Kit watched her closely. "I will help you," he said again, as if to encourage her.

She nodded, whispering to him, "I have a healing spell. I do not know if it's strong enough—"

"*Try it.*"

"I will. But these Habaddon men are not accustomed to sorcery. They may be fearful, and I cannot be interrupted."

"I will watch over you."

So Lanyon placed her palms one atop the other on Bennek's forehead and, closing her eyes, she began a soft chant.

Pantheren had been heading outside to see that the watch was set, but when he heard Lanyon's voice he turned back. "Lanyon! What spell do you work on him?"

Kit rose to his feet, shooting a warning glance at Jakurian, who had turned to look. "Leave her in peace! She seeks to save him."

"Save him how?" Pantheren demanded. "Lanyon, answer me!"

"It's a healing spell," Kit said. "You know she would not harm him."

Pantheren was not satisfied. "Lanyon, even the Snow Chanter does not know how to heal . . . though Édan does. Marshal told me what you saw in the thickets. Édan is cursed, isn't he? Just as Jahallon is cursed. I will not let you heal Bennek in that way."

Kit stepped toward Pantheren, a fist clenched in anger, but he hesitated when he heard Lanyon's soft voice begin to tremble. He looked at her.

They all waited, to see if she would speak.

Lanyon kept on to the end of a long verse of syllables. Then she stopped her chant. Her eyes opened. She fixed a bitter gaze on Pantheren. "You think I would do such a thing?"

"Why did you tell us Édan was dead?"

"Because he was! Yes, Siddél has cursed him, but I did not know it until today."

"There are other things you have not told us."

"I confess this is true, and I promise I will tell you everything that happened that night—but not now. Please, War Father." Her gaze lowered, to fix on Bennek's waxen face. "I think he does not have much time, and I am already tired."

"Let her try," Kit insisted.

Pantheren did not look convinced, but he nodded reluctantly. "Very well. But do not reach farther than you can . . . or farther than you should."

There was much coming and going throughout the afternoon as the men took turns in the bathhouse. Gear was sorted, swords sharpened, and supper prepared. Soft words were traded with the wounded. None of this touched Lanyon. Her chant persisted in unvarying rhythm.

In the evening, Tayeraisa came in and listened for a time. Then she went out again, seeming thoughtful.

As darkness gathered, Kaliel lay awake beside the fire, the pain of his injured leg oddly distant. For some time he listened to Lanyon's voice. Then he turned to his wounded companions. "Can you feel that?" he wondered aloud. "Bahir? Alhimbra? Can you feel a current moving in the Mere?"

"I can," Alhimbra said. "It's a subtle thing, with a sweetness to it. It gives me ease."

"It's a seduction," Bahir countered. He cast a suspicious gaze at Lanyon. "There is too much that is strange in this place. I fear we will lose our way."

"Sorcery is an Inyomere art," Alhimbra acknowledged. "But it is not always evil."

Kaliel nodded his agreement. "Even in Habaddon there is sorcery. Jahallon himself has the gift of farseeing."

"That is not sorcery," Bahir countered. "Jahallon had his gift before the people were tainted by the Inyomere of the Wild."

"Speak gently, Bahir," Alhimbra urged. "For the Samokeäns love their Snow Chanter. Even Jakurian proudly claims his descent."

"I do not speak against Samokea," Bahir said. "But sorcery is the art of the Inyomere and I will never trust it."

Marshal volunteered to take the first watch that night, but Pantheren said they would share it.

The night was cold and fog-bound, with nothing to be seen but darkness all around.

"Kina will patrol the field," Pantheren said. "You and I will watch with our ears."

At first they stood on the porch. Marshal heard the chatter of the stream, the stamp of the horses, the blur of soft conversation from the house. Mostly he listened for Lanyon's faint voice, chanting endless rounds of words that had no meaning that he knew. Finally he could bear it no longer. "I can hear nothing but our own noise. Let us walk about."

"If you can see to put one step in front of another, you can see more than me."

"Let us call Kina, then. Darkness is nothing to her."

So they summoned Kina and she led them across the bridge. There they heard the sound of their boots in the wet grass and now and then the call of some lonely night bird.

"I am tired," Pantheren said at last. "More tired than I can ever remember being. It's said men weaken if they are allowed to grow old. Perhaps it's true."

"There is no sleep in me," Marshal answered.

"You are haunted by this day."

Marshal said nothing to this.

"Why have you not been into the house to see your brother?" Pantheren asked him.

"I cannot look on him," Marshal admitted. "I cannot bear it."

"Because you blame yourself for it."

"It is my fault. I let it happen."

"And did you imagine you could protect him always?"

"Sir, you misunderstand me. I have not such a high regard for myself. Not even Jahallon could guarantee the life of any man. But Bennek did not fall in battle. I asked him to confound the arowl—"

"It was I who asked him, Marshal."

"And he was reluctant, but I made him do it. Sir, he is helpless when he works that spell. I promised I would watch over him . . . but he did not trust me to do it. He put his weapons close at hand, saying I might become distracted. He knew I would fail. He foresaw it."

"He understood the chaos of battle, Marshal. That is all. We were in a desperate fight. Jakurian spoke truly when he said that he and his men would all be consumed now if Bennek had not confounded the pack. You did as much as any man could."

"And still Bennek lies on his deathbed."

Pantheren sighed in the darkness. "Marshal, if you had wanted him to remain unharmed you should have sent him south to Hallah when he was still a small boy. But that you could not do, for Bennek is a warrior of the north, and if he dies, he will die as a warrior. It is the same for all of us. On the day we are born our mothers know what our ends will be. It does not fall to us to ask why one man lives, when another makes the crossing. That is known only to the One who wakened us, if it is known at all. Our duty is to defend the Wild and our place in it. We must vanquish the blasphemy of Siddél so that the Wild may flourish again. Put aside your guilt, for it weakens you. You are an honorable man, with many tasks left to do before you make your own crossing."

Marshal made no answer to this, but when the watch was done he went into the house. Kit had fallen asleep at Bennek's side, but Lanyon still sat at his head, chanting now in a hoarse whisper.

Marshal put more wood on the fire. Then he sat beside his brother and listened to his soft breathing, weighing again what Pantheren had said and letting himself feel the truth of it. He kissed Bennek's hand. "I am not sad," he said, "for all will be set right when we cross over."

"But when you are all gone away, I will still be here."

He looked up, surprised to see Tayeraisa. The firelight cast a warm glow on her skin that reminded him of the flush of dawn among the peaks. "Blessed One, I did not mean we would abandon you."

"Still, it is true time will take you away. But though you are gone, the Wild will remain. Do not leave it a broken thing! It is the duty of the people, of *my* people, to rid the Wild of the evil of the arowl. Do not flee this task."

"Far Mother, we will serve you in this, for as long as fate allows."

"I know you will, and Kit and Bennek too."

"Bennek would serve you longer if he could."

"Does he not look better to you?" She stepped around Kit's sleeping figure to crouch beside Lanyon, who showed no awareness of her. "My little sister has done much for him this night, though she is weary now. Her will fades. But I have learned the name of this spell, and I will call it until the dawn. Take Lanyon to sleep now, for she is at the end of her strength."

Hope woke in Marshal's heart. He scrambled to his feet. "My far mother, never will I forget this kindness."

"Never will I forget your faith."

She held her hands poised above Bennek's forehead, setting them on his brow when Marshal lifted Lanyon's hands away. Tayeraisa took up the chant, while Lanyon crumpled in Marshal's arms.

He carried her to the corner where she had left her things, and he covered her in a blanket. Then finally he gave into sleep himself, drifting away to the soft, strong music of Tayeraisa's voice.

# 18

THE SUN SHONE bright that morning. The shutters were thrown open. Adrift between waking and dreams, Bennek felt the pressure of light on his closed eyes and imagined himself as thistledown lofted high above the land on a gentle breeze. Only slowly did the sounds around him bring him back into the world: the soft prattle of the men, their footsteps as they came and went, the breathy voice of the fire, the sizzle of breakfast cooking.

A soft hand touched his cheek. "You are wakeful," Lanyon said happily. He felt her lips warm against his ear as she whispered, "Bennek, I know you hear me. You must thrive, for I need you to be well. Do not break my heart."

A heavier hand rested on his forehead. "His fever is all but gone," Pantheren announced. "And his breathing has eased." Bennek felt the touch of cool air as the blanket that covered him was lifted aside. "Even the swelling in his leg has subsided. You have called him back to life, Lanyon."

"He has much life in him, do you not, Bennek?"

Bennek did not remember how to make an answer, but Lanyon touched his cheek again, saying, "Do not fret. You will be well soon, and then I will teach you the fire spell, as I promised."

"He is a good man," Pantheren said in humor. "Do not corrupt him with magic." Then came the sound of his footsteps moving away to the other side of the fire.

Bennek could not tell if Lanyon was still beside him until he blinked. Then, a gentle hand wiped his eyes with a damp cloth. The door opened. Bennek glimpsed Jakurian with a blaze of sunlight behind him, before squeezing his eyes shut against the glare.

"Ah, Lanyon Kyramanthes," Jakurian said in a hushed voice, "how does Bennek fare?"

She answered merrily, from somewhere just out of sight, "He is well, War Father . . . considering."

"All thanks to the spell worked by you and the Snow Chanter. It has filled this house with wholesomeness. Infection has not touched the wounds of any man here. Pain has been eased, fever quenched, and while I should be sore in every limb, I feel refreshed, as if with many days of rest."

From the other side of the fire, Kaliel said, "I am pleased to hear it, my captain." He had passed a quiet night despite the grave wounds on his calf and thigh. "Let us then return all the sooner to our homes. This sorcerer we pursued is dead and his arowl are slain. Our task here is done."

Bennek blinked and looked up. The Habaddon captain loomed above him, looking surprised at Kaliel's words, then puzzled, when the other men in the house swiftly voiced their agreement.

Jakurian said to them, "I confess it has not been in my mind to turn back so soon. I have seen wonders in Samokea and I have heard mention of more. As for the sorcerer, I think his fate is not certain, and neither is his name."

Sleep tugged at Bennek. His eyes fluttered closed. He only half-listened to Jakurian as the captain told his men, "There is a strange story unfolding here. This morning I asked Kit what had brought him north, and he said it was first to rescue the Snow Chanter, and now that is accomplished, to slay Siddél.

"To slay Siddél! I have never had the temerity to even imagine such a thing, but Kit speaks of it so matter-of-factly I begin to believe it's possible . . . especially when I hear Pantheren has given his support to the deed. Tell us, War Father, do you truly see hope in it?"

Bennek was startled back to full awareness by Pantheren's

sharp response. "It is not a question of hope. It is only a deed we must try."

"So it *is* true." Jakurian sounded pleased. "Pantheren of Habaddon has resolved to meet the monster in his lair."

"I am the one resolved to it," Lanyon said softly.

Bennek opened his eyes to look for her, but she was still behind him. He could not see her, though he could see Jakurian looking on her with a thoughtful gaze. "There is a strange story here," he said again. "I think we should hear it in full before judging if our task in Samokea is done."

"Summon the men," Pantheren said. "I would hear the full story too."

Bennek tried to stay awake, but the sounds around him blurred and for a time nightmares flitted through his mind. In these visions it was night. He heard the rumble of thunder, and Siddél's mocking voice on a storm wind. In a dark bedchamber the only light came from a stray flame flickering on a hearth. In that faint glimmer he saw a woman waking with a start. He could not see her face but he knew it was Lanyon. She had gone to sleep with her babies beside her but now the bed was empty.

A touch of gentle fingers against his cheek brought him back to awareness. He heard again the sounds of the cottage: water boiling on the stove, Kina pacing the porch, and Lanyon speaking in a soft, reluctant voice. "From that chamber a stairway went up to Édan's study. The door to it stood open just a little and around its edge a blue-gold light flickered—"

Her breathing was ragged with fear as she raced up that staircase. The door opened easily, and in silence. She looked in on a long table covered in blue and gold flames. No heat could be felt from the burning. This was not a natural fire. Smoke rose from it as a shimmering vapor, like unformed ghosts. She stepped closer . . .

Bennek again felt Lanyon's fingers, light against his cheek, and once more the night receded. Daylight pressed against his closed eyes.

Lanyon asked the listening men, "If a warrior dies a shameful death, do you describe his cowardice to the widow who loves him? Or do you tell her he was a brave man who did his best?"

Pantheren answered her. "No one goes forever untouched by fear. We remember the best of a man."

She said, "I know Jahallon loved Édan. He loves him still. Édan's deeds still inspire men. He is the pride of Samokea. So when Jahallon and Pantheren came upon me this summer, I did not tell them all that I knew of that night. Let Édan be loved! That's what I thought. No good could be served by soiling his memory . . . and in truth I was ashamed that anyone should know what really happened.

"But now Édan is alive, and you, War Father, and these men, and Jahallon—all of you!—before you seek him out and beg him to again ride at the head of your armies, *know this*—"

Bennek gasped as darkness closed in on him again. Blue-gold fire shimmered and danced on the table top. And, half-hidden within the flames, he saw them: the infant cradled in the small boy's embrace. Not burning. No, they were *fading*, transforming slowly into a shimmering vapor. A single arrow pierced through both their hearts, its shaft carved with prayers and the emergent arrowhead beaded with droplets of blood like red sweat.

On the other side of the table, gazing at Lanyon across the fire, was Édan, his face youthful and unscarred. "They were born to war," he said gently. "They were born to the service of the people."

Then Bennek fell away into a deeper darkness and far away he heard a woman screaming, but Édan spoke close beside him: "I have sacrificed what I love only to end this war."

The blue-gold fire licked away the last evidence of Lanyon's children, leaving only the arrow behind.

The night went silent.

Édan set the arrow against the string of a heavy bow. He gazed up another staircase, one leading past a wooden door to the roof. He stood there for several heartbeats, waiting for his enemy to come. Then all the dogs in the city howled as a blast of lightning blew the door to splinters.

Édan drew his bow, but Siddél did not come just yet. Instead, a second stroke of lightning exploded against the rafters. Part of the roof collapsed. At the same time all the books and furnishings, the wall hangings and the curtains, burst into flame.

Again came the comfort of Lanyon's touch, but this time the darkness did not recede.

"You have heard of Édan's voice?" she asked the men. "He could speak as the Inyomere do with one another—silently, within the mind. So he spoke to me then. The roof had fallen in on him. He lay crushed and dying beneath the heavy beams. He told me, silently, to find his cursed arrow. He passed this task to *me*! And Siddél came. I saw him beyond the flames. I was afraid, and I retreated to the inner door.

*Grathrak!*

Bennek flinched as the Inyomere's deafening voice spoke this single word and all the fires died. Choking black smoke filled the chamber. Nothing could be seen. Then a rush of wind stirred the smoke and there was a great clash and clatter.

Lanyon said, "I aimed Édan's arrow at the noise. I guided the flight of the spell it carried so it would not go astray. But it turned out that Édan was in the way."

From across the room, Bennek saw an enchanted flame flare around the arrow's feathers, illuminating its victim. The arrow had struck Édan in the chest as he hung suspended by his hair in the great fist of the Inyomere Siddél, who was so tall he hunched beneath the broken rafters.

Édan was certainly dead. Bennek could not doubt it.

Then the darkness drew away and daylight took over. Bennek blinked, seeing again the cottage, crowded with men.

Lanyon said, "I think Siddél sensed his peril. It may even be that the arrow pricked him when it passed through Édan, for he dropped Édan's body and fled howling through the broken roof. I pulled the arrow from Édan's chest. The arrowhead does not have hooks and it came out cleanly—but he did not gasp or flinch. War Father, I swear to you he was dead! *You* would have thought him dead.

"I could not flee, for the room below was on fire. I could not breathe for all the smoke and the heat—and I heard Siddél returning, on the stairway to the roof—returning for Édan. I know that now."

She shook her head. "I didn't know what else to do, except to speak the spell of time that Édan had taught to me. But I was enlivened with a power that was not my own, and I also held Édan's arrow in my hands. The spell came with a force I never imagined possible, and it carried me through all the years since that night."

Again she touched Bennek's cheek. "Be at rest," she whispered. "I will say no more on it."

Pantheren looked around the cottage and saw his own astonishment and horror reflected on the faces of the men. It seemed to him it should have been dark night, but the morning remained bright.

He returned his gaze to Lanyon. "Something of life must have been left in Édan when Siddél returned. I have seen it before—mortally wounded men holding on past all expectation."

"So it's true then," Jakurian mused. "Édan is still in the world. Siddél must have taken him, and cursed him. But how did he escape the monster?"

Bahir said, "No doubt he corrupted the arowl that guarded him. Aidin or Édan—he could command the arowl to do what he required."

Pantheren walked to a window; he looked out on the fields. "Siddél did not even know Édan had escaped him—the great blundering fool!—until he discovered him yesterday."

Jakurian joined him. "Siddél knows now. He will hunt Édan. It will be dangerous for him to move about, even with dire wolves to protect him. Why didn't he return to my father? As Lanyon has said, his name is well-loved in Habaddon. He would have been embraced as a hero."

"He is ashamed," Pantheren said. "He spent the lives of his children, he failed to defend the Citadel of the Snow Chanter, he lost Samokea—and all for nothing, because Siddél still lives. The shame must burn in him."

"You think he is capable of feeling shame?" Lanyon demanded. All turned to look at her.

"It's not shame that drives him. He is *not* ashamed of what he did. He believes he made a great sacrifice and we should love him for it. No, it is something else that drives him. Kit! Marshal—do you remember what happened when I used the arrow to break the ice that held the Snow Chanter?"

They both looked confused, but Tayeraisa answered. "The cold of the ice followed the spell's path back to you. I felt it."

"Yes. The arrow drinks from its victims and some of that power it keeps, but the rest rolls back to the archer. Yesterday Édan said to me these words, *'You have taken enough from me already.'* I am remembering how I felt that night after the arrow killed him. I was flush with power. *His* power, drained from him by the spell of the arrow.

"Yesterday, Édan stopped me from slaying Siddél. He spoiled my shot. And he said to me, *'It is not for you to become the storm.'* War Father, do you understand? It is not his wish just to end the Long War, just to see Siddél destroyed—"

"He would become the storm," Jakurian said. "He would take for himself the power of Siddél."

Bahir added, "And him a man who would murder his own children."

Lanyon nodded. "I will not let him have the talisman. It is not his task anymore."

Afterward, Lanyon helped Bennek to eat some porridge, while the other men went out to enjoy the sun. Before long, Kit came in through the back door, bringing Kina with him. The hound went straight to Bennek, lying next to him with her chin resting on his pallet.

"She has been so worried for you," Lanyon told him. "I think she is happy now."

She watched Bennek try to smile, though it came out as a grimace.

"Ah, Bennek," Kit chided, "you should not make such faces at a pretty woman."

Bennek's eyes closed, and Kit signaled Lanyon to step away. "Plans are being made outside," he whispered. "Pantheren wants to talk to you."

She left Kit and Kina to watch, returning just a few minutes later. "They are coming," she warned.

Kit rose and shooed Kina out the back door. A moment later the front door opened and Pantheren came in with Marshal.

"We will tell him now," Marshal announced.

Lanyon nodded. They all sat together around Bennek. Lanyon took his hand, rousing him from sleep.

He looked at her and smiled—a pretty smile this time—but then he noticed the others. He did not like what he saw on their faces.

"Bennek, we are going on tomorrow," Marshal told him. "The land has been mostly emptied of arowl, so there's a chance we may journey far unhindered—but we must go at once, before more come over the mountains."

Pantheren wanted the full truth out. "Bennek, you will go south with Jakurian's men."

Bennek understood now what they intended. He whispered a hoarse, "*No.*" He tried to sit up, but he could not. Lanyon eased him back to the pillow.

"Jakurian's men will care for you," Pantheren went on gently, remorselessly. "They will bring you safely to Habaddon. You cannot ride, so you must return by the river. The Snow Chanter has promised to provide us a boat. The horses will follow on the shore."

"No," Bennek whispered. "I must go on. You will need me."

Marshal took his hand. "We *will* need you. But we will have to make do just the same. Jakurian will come with us—"

"*No.*" Bennek tried to sit up again, and again he failed. "Marshal, do not send me away. A few days rest, and I will be well."

"There is no choice in it," Pantheren said with finality. "It will take many times more than a few days for you to heal. When you are well though, you may offer your oath to Jahallon. Then Bennek, I think you will see enough battles to satisfy even your warrior's heart."

They stayed one more night, but on the next morning they bade the Snow Chanter farewell. Kit pleaded with her to come north with them, but she declined. "I must return to the peaks and dwell there until the winter has filled me and I am myself again." But she stayed to watch them as they set out over the field.

Four men went on foot, carrying Bennek's litter. All the others went on horseback. It was three miles through the grasslands to the River Talahnon. Here the river slowed after its sprint from the mountain, and among the reeds they found two canoes as the Snow Chanter had promised.

Jakurian had his men test the canoes. While they were on the water, five of the horses were unsaddled.

The canoes passed muster and returned to the riverbank, where they were loaded with the saddles and supplies of those who would go on. It was the work of a few minutes to cross the river and unload the cargo on the other bank. Then the canoes returned.

The moment of parting had come. Jakurian spoke quietly with his men, while Marshal and Kit tried to comfort Bennek as they could. The vigor that had only begun to return to him had drained away, and he seemed stricken with a terrible sadness, so that Marshal feared again for his survival. "You must not grieve, Bennek. We will be together again, in this world or the next."

"I am not grieving," Bennek said to him in a whisper. "I never am sad. I only hope that you will come back someday."

Marshal kissed his forehead. Then he turned quickly away.

Kit squeezed Bennek's hand. "You must represent us well in Habaddon, my cousin. Remember that Pantheron said the captains thought us somewhat odd and addled. You must not disappoint them!"

"I will try to live up to your example."

"There's my lad." Kit started to rise.

"Where is Lanyon?" Bennek asked him.

Kit looked around, and discovered her standing at the water's edge, gazing across the river, with Kina at her side. He sighed. "I think she is not sad, like you."

As if sensing his gaze, Lanyon turned, her coppery hair blowing in long ribbons about her face.

"Take care, Bennek," Kit said.

"And you," he whispered. Then he was alone, but only for a moment. Next he knew, Lanyon was kneeling beside him. He reached up, past the blowing strands of her hair to touch her cheek. "You are here."

She smiled. Then she caught his hand, and kissed it. "You will thrive, Bennek."

"You must come back and teach me the fire spell."

"Do you remember the chant I spoke over you?"

He nodded.

"That is a better magic. Practice that instead."

She started to rise, but he gripped her hand more tightly. "Take the pendant from around my neck. I want you to have it." With his other hand he started to reach for the leather thong that bound it, but the pain from his ribs made him cry out.

"Bennek stop!" She cupped both his hands to restrain him.

"Please wear it, Lanyon. Let me be with you still."

She shook her head. "It's your mother's and it belongs with you."

"You will forget me," he said in sudden anger.

She looked on him with a wistful smile. "No, I do not think I will." Then she was away, running down to the canoes.

Finally it was only Kina who waited at his side. Bennek scratched her ear and stroked her head. Then Pantheren whistled for her to come. At first she did not listen. So Pantheren called her again, and then a third time. Finally, Bennek told her she must go.

The horses were driven into the water. They swam across the river behind the canoes and Kina swam with them.

After a time, the canoes returned. Bennek was laid in one, with saddle blankets to pad his head and back. Gear was stowed around him. A man named Meriton had the task of handling the canoe. "Are you ready, son?" he asked Bennek.

"I am ready," Bennek assured him.

It was only the brightness of the sun in the noontime sky that made his eyes water.

On the north bank, no one hurried.

They left the horses unsaddled so that they might roll in the grass and sun themselves after their river crossing, but the animals took no ease. They shifted restlessly, tugging at their ropes and neighing loudly to their friends left behind across the river. Kina shared their mood. She trotted back and forth, back and forth, at the water's edge, her gaze fixed on the canoe where Bennek rested.

"You would do well to leash her," Jakurian advised, but Pantheren made no answer. No one else spoke.

Across the river, Alhimbra and Kaliel were assisted into the second canoe. Then the boats were launched. On shore, those five who would ride mounted their horses. They waved a final goodbye, calling out good wishes that were mostly caught on the wind and carried away. Then they set out south and east along the river, following behind the boats.

Kina could bear it no longer. With a frantic yelp she leaped into the water and set out downriver, swimming hard with the current at her back.

Lanyon started forward in shock. "Kina! Ki-*na!*" The hound refused to hear. Lanyon turned to Pantheren, to find him watching the dog with a cold gaze. "War Father, you must call her back before she has gone so far she cannot hear you!"

Pantheren shook his head. "Bennek is her master now." He turned his back on the river. "Jakurian, Marshal, Kit—our task lies before us. Let us ready the horses."

Lanyon left them the work of grooming and saddling the animals. She stayed by the river's edge, watching Kina until, far down the river, the dog reached the southern bank and vanished into the tall grass. A moment later the canoes, tiny with distance, disappeared from sight. The horsemen had become dark specks that bobbed and floated in a steady retreat into the green, until finally they too were swallowed by the vastness of the plain.

Marshal brought the mare that had been given to Lanyon to ride. "Lanyon? All is ready."

"Then let us find Siddél," she said softly, "as we found the Snow Chanter."

For most of that afternoon they rode in silence, with the foothills of the Tiyat-kel on their left, and the lush grasslands reaching to the eastern horizon. They saw rabbit and pheasant, and once they came across the burrow of a fox. They saw no living arowl, but they passed the remains of the beasts: broken skulls, scattered bones, and poorly made weapons rusting under the open sky.

"The bones look gnawed," Kit observed. "Perhaps they consume one another?"

"I have little doubt of it," Jakurian answered. "Though such appetites are forgotten if ever they catch the scent of the people."

In the evening they made camp beside a small stream that came down from the foothills. They made no fire.

NEXT IN THE WILD TRILOGY

BOOK II

# The Long War

BY LINDA NAGATA

From Mythic Island Press LLC
Learn more at MythicIslandPress.com

Made in the USA
Monee, IL
14 January 2022